BOOK 3 OF MORNA'S LEGACY

LOVE BEYOND HOPE

A SCOTTISH TIME TRAVELING ROMANCE

BETHANY CLAIRE

For Mo

Chapter 1

Austin, TX

Present Day

Two thoughts flashed through my mind as my trembling fingers gripped at the letter and the set of keys my husband extended in my direction. The first was that if Brian said one more word, I planned to take off my shoe and ram the pointy end of the heel deep into his skull. The second was that I was so ashamed at my own stupidity, I was nearly just as inclined to ram the heel of the other shoe into my own head.

How could I have let so many months pass with him making the most ridiculous excuses to stay away from home without catching on? What a silly, desperate fool I must have been to make it so easy for him to break his vows. I'm sure he'd been thrilled to marry such an unassuming, trusting wife.

Now that I knew, over a year's worth of clues seemed blaringly obvious. While we'd never truly been happy, I never thought him capable of such a betrayal. He was an ass to be sure, but a cheat, a liar? I'd not seen this in him.

I had time to come to terms with his affair, weeks of lawyer negotiations and packing my belongings quickly made me glad to be rid of him, but what had me shaking with anger and unshed tears was the revelation of the new information I held in my hand.

"Are you really so surprised? What else would Bri have done with the house after she moved? She left too quickly to sell the place, and it's not like she had that many friends. Why shouldn't I have used it?"

I squeezed the key so tightly that its ridges buried deep into my hand, indenting the skin. I was sure he could see the steam coming out of my ears, but I refused to scream at him as he expected. Brian would call it another one of my "ginger" moments and be sure to tell me it was another reason I'd driven him into the affair. I would not give him the satisfaction.

"No," I said the word calmly and slowly released my breath so that it didn't come out as a loud sigh of frustration. "I'm not surprised at all, I'd just never given it much thought. What I'm surprised about is how you thought it was okay to keep this letter from me. This is not addressed to you."

He chuckled once before speaking, and I ground my heel into the floor to keep myself from ripping it off and attacking him.

"You're right. It isn't, but we were married when it came in the mail and what's yours is mine, yes? Besides, Leah and I needed somewhere to go. It's not like we could come back here when you were always sitting in the house waiting on me."

My face could not have grown any hotter, but still I did not raise my voice. "You can justify anything can't you? Bri would strangle you herself if she knew you'd been staying there."

Turning from him, I walked across the room to swing the last of my belongings, all thrown messily into a large duffle bag, over my shoulder so that I could make my way out of the door. I'd not even read the letter yet. As soon as I saw Bri Conall's handwriting and the key tucked inside the envelope, I knew that my friend had left her house in my care. The date at the top showed just how long Brian had kept this from me.

There was so much more that I could say to him, so much more I wanted to say, but I knew none of it would do any good. He would never see the kind of man he was, and I was tired of him, of everything really. I only wanted to get out of this house without saying another word. I didn't ever want to see him again.

"I wasn't the only one who cheated. Maybe you didn't do it in person, but in mind you did. Every time I held you, I could see *him* behind your eyes. It's too bad for you really. He didn't want you either. That's why you ran to me, isn't it?"

He spoke to my back and I didn't respond. If only Brian would let me be and not say anything else, I might be able to make it out of the room and to my car without bursting into tears. I knew he wouldn't be so kind.

"She's nuts. She rambles on in the letter about you coming to visit her at the castle and how much you would love the seventeenth century. Bri's completely out of her mind. No wonder you two were such good friends."

I kept my back to him as I reached for the door handle, and I swallowed the lump in my throat as he chuckled once more. "Goodbye, Brian." I didn't look back as I walked out the door, started the engine, and pulled out of the driveway as quickly as I could.

In the rearview mirror I could see his mistress, Leah, pulling into the driveway, replacing my spot in our home so quickly it was as if I'd never been there. I couldn't bring myself to feel any hatred toward her. Only pity. God help her, the poor girl had no idea what she'd gotten herself into.

*   *   *

3

As much as I didn't want to spend the night at Bri's old home, especially after learning what Brian used it for, it relieved me to be able to cancel my hotel reservations. Classroom teachers made little. As a teacher's aide, I made even less. I couldn't move into my new apartment for another week, and with no family to stay with until then, I had no choice but to reserve a room at the shabbiest of hotels.

If it meant saving a little money, I could push away the memories that would flood me in Bri's old home - - Brian's lovenest. Memories of nights spent with Brian when we'd been dating, before he sold the home to my friend. Memories of helping Bri paint and work away in the old bachelor pad until it was beautiful and perfect, just as she wished it. It's not as if I planned on sleeping much anyway.

The flowers on the front porch that she tended to so carefully had long since died, and an uncomfortable pang knocked on my heart at the thought of how much I missed Bri. I still didn't fully understand what happened to her. She was the classroom teacher, and I worked directly under her. She was also the closest friend I'd ever had. When she disappeared after accompanying her archaeologist mother on a dig in Scotland, it's no stretch to say that I lost it a little.

When I finally found her after flying to Scotland, it was clear that she'd fallen madly in love. I saw how much her new husband, Eoin, adored her, and I couldn't blame her a bit for leaving everything behind. I would've done the same.

I'd experienced love like that once, but it hadn't been with Brian. What he said to me was true. The loss of the man that came before him, Jep, led me to settle for Brian.

I understood the love thing. What I didn't understand was why Bri lied to me about it. She lied so confidently, weaving a story so detailed that I truly did want to believe her, but I couldn't. People do not, and she did not, travel through time.

Anxious to read her letter, I turned the key and stepped inside the entryway. To my surprise, the place was immaculate. Well, at least the front part of the house was. Most likely, only one area of the house had been regularly used, and I would stay clear of that room.

I dropped my bag in the doorway, carrying only the letter into the living room with me as I slowly made my way around the room turning on the lights and lighting a few candles.

Once the room was properly lit and the smell of pumpkin-scented candles wafted sweetly through the air, I went into the kitchen and started water heating so that I could steep a large cup of tea. I was in desperate need of anything to soothe my frazzled nerves and angry heart.

It had been weeks since I'd slept properly. Now that the divorce was final and I was gone from Brian's life, all of the stress, sadness, anxiety, and insomnia of the past days seemed to hit me at once.

After the kettle whistled and I poured the steaming water over a large cup filled with several tea bags, I all but collapsed onto the oversized sofa that sat in the middle of the living room. I reached out and felt for a coaster. After placing the cup of tea on it, I propped pillows up behind me so that I could sit up to read the letter.

I was incredibly curious to read its contents. I'd not heard a word from her since the wedding. She'd not even taken the time to say goodbye, slipping away during the middle of the reception. I was angry with her for that, but I supposed Bri had her reasons. And she did leave me a house which certainly counted for something, not that she could've known just how much I would need it. Or perhaps she had, and that was the very reason she left it for me. She'd never really liked Brian.

I didn't need to open the envelope. Brian had already done that, and the rumpled edges showed just how many times he read it through himself, clearly trying to make sense of Bri's words.

It was short and, while I could easily see that the handwriting was Bri's, it looked hurried, as if her idea to write the letter had been a last minute thought before she returned to Scotland. The first part of the letter was what I'd expected, an apology for leaving so suddenly and an explanation that the house was now mine to use as I saw fit. She spoke of how much she loved me, how much my friendship meant to her and, as Brian said, she spoke of how much she loved life in the seventeenth century and that she believed I would love it, too.

After that, she changed subjects quickly, only writing a few sentences at the bottom of the page. She'd not even bothered to sign her name.

> *"The house is yours while you need it, Mitsy, but when it comes time for you to get away and you're ready to start a new life, come and find me. You're welcome here. You will need the help of the innkeepers you met in Scotland. I'm not going to bother trying to tell you what happened again. I know you didn't believe me last time, and I don't expect you would believe me now...not until you experience it. Call them when you're ready."*

I flung my feet over the edge of the couch and turned, suddenly needing a large gulp of tea. I stared down at the odd words with fascination. She didn't even state it as if it were a question that I would need to leave here, she wrote it as if she knew that I would. Not only that, it suddenly seemed to me that perhaps she didn't intentionally lie. She actually believed what she said.

That changed things and made me worry for her even more. Even after I found Bri and she told me the elaborate tale, even after I met Blaire, the woman who so closely resembled her that I was certain they had to be related in some manner, I still could not believe my friend's story. There was a reason she felt the need to lie and, frankly, I was so glad to know that Bri was alive and not murdered and laying in a ditch in the middle of Scotland that I decided to let it go. Begrudgingly, I'd accepted the fact that I would never know the truth of what happened to her after she disappeared, but if she truly believed that she'd traveled back in time then something terrible happened to her.

Her brain was addled, disturbed, and I owed it to her to find out just what and who had done this to her. Not that I didn't need to get away from this place for personal reasons, I certainly did, but a trip to Scotland to find Bri once again and try and talk her out of her delusions would be the perfect excuse to leave. Better to help someone out of a problem than to wade in the self-pity I felt at my own.

Moving back to the front doorway, I reached into my duffle bag to withdraw my wallet and cell phone where I'd saved the phone number for the strange innkeepers I'd tracked down during my search for Bri. They'd been nearly impossible to get ahold of, and I was not altogether sure that I'd be able to reach them again. I got the impression that their phone number and address were not readily available.

I clicked the call button as quickly as I could, not waiting a moment so that I could change my mind. The phone rang once and then was answered by the unmistakable voice of the innkeeper herself.

"Why, Mitsy, how are ye, dear? Jerry and I have been expecting a call from ye any minute. I suggest that ye start packing up yer things, though ye willna need much once ye get here."

My mouth hung open. How did she know who called? I doubted that she had caller ID in the little inn. How did she know that I planned on coming there? I'd yet to say a word on the phone, and I didn't know what to say now. "Um…hi. Why would you expect a call from me?"

The old woman at the other end of the phone laughed softly before speaking again. "Well, dear, I know a large number of things that I doubt ye would expect me to. Best ye get yerself here and then I will tell ye more. Though I'm sure ye willna believe a bit of it until ye see it for yerself."

She was certainly right about that. "Ok…uh, is Bri there? May I speak to her for a moment?"

I knew she would tell me she wasn't there, but obviously she was. How else would the woman have known that Bri suggested I come there?

"Ye know that she isna here, love. She's a far time away from here to be sure, but ye will see her soon enough. She told me to tell ye when ye called that she doesna wish for ye to pay for yer plane ticket on yer own. She knows your budget is limited. I've already called the airline and purchased a ticket for ye. Yer flight is at 3:00 p.m. tomorrow. All ye need to do is check-in at the counter. Yer rental car has been arranged as well. I suppose since ye found yer way to our inn once before, ye are capable of doing it again. We will see ye soon. Safe travels, Mitsy."

She hung up the phone, and I stared at the wall in confusion. Thank God it was summer. As long as I didn't stay gone for more than a month, I wouldn't have to make arrangements with work.

It seemed that by this time tomorrow, I would find myself on a flight headed to Scotland.

Chapter 2

Baodan McMillan glanced in Niall's direction, the two brothers' eyes locking at the suspicion he knew they both felt at their mother's words. She was leaving McMillan Castle, the home she'd known for over three decades.

He could make no sense of it, the sudden announcement. She fell ill nearly a month ago and, with each passing day, she grew weaker. It did not sit well with him that his mother had decided to find a home elsewhere. The people in their territory would not understand it, and he wished to be near her so that he could help care for her during her sickness.

Leaning across the dining hall table, he wrapped his fingers around both her hands, squeezing them gently. "Are ye saying that ye wish to go on a journey, Mother? Ye must know that ye are too weak, but surely it would do ye some good to escape the castle walls for a while, aye? If ye wish, I shall take ye for a ride so that ye may spend the afternoon away from the castle tomorrow."

Baodan glanced up to see Niall nod at him across the table, showing his approval at the suggestion. Out of the corner of his eye he could see Eoghanan, his youngest brother, whose red hair and pale face were so different from his own dark brown wavy curls or Niall's ink-colored tendrils. It labeled him as the outcast he was. He looked down angrily, and Baodan knew he would speak up in disagreement.

"No, Baodan. It willna do for her to only leave here for a short while. She needs to reside elsewhere. She wishes it."

Boadan's teeth ground together as he gripped the edge of the table with his free hand. "I doona think that is for ye to say, Eoghanan." He started to continue but stopped as his mother pulled on his hand.

"I willna allow ye to speak to him so, I doona care how old ye are. He is right. I shall be leaving to reside elsewhere for the foreseeable future. I leave in the morning."

Baodan stood, unable to sit calmly. How could his mother allow Eoghanan to influence her so? Of all her sons, she heeded the words of the one who had betrayed him, causing him to lose the person dearest to him. He paced the room, circling the table where his mother and two brothers sat. He knew he would be unable to change her mind, but he'd be damned if he allowed her to make the journey without him. "Where is it that ye plan on going, Mother? Ye do know how unusual this is of ye, aye? Who will care for ye?"

"I miss me sister. Too much time has passed since I have seen her. She resides in a private cottage on the grounds of Cameron Castle and has done so ever since her husband passed away. She has invited me to live with her, and I shall. She says they have a talented healer in their territory. I suspect she will have me feeling better in due time. Ye doona need me to run the keep, and I will be but a three day journey from ye all. While I am ill and, until I have grandchildren that need spoiling, I doona see a reason to stay here tending over ye three boys like ye are all too young to tend for yerselves, and I doona wish for any of ye to tend over me."

Baodan hadn't realized he held his breath until he exhaled, softening his resolve as he moved to sit by his mother once again. His worry for her expressed itself through frustration, and he knew she didn't deserve such treatment from him. "I appreciate yer confidence in us Mother, but we all still depend on ye much more than we realize. I know that I willna change yer mind, though I canna say that I think it a good idea. At the verra least, I will travel with ye and see ye safely settled."

His mother spoke quickly, too quickly, and it only served to increase his suspicions. "No. Eoghanan has already agreed to travel with me. There is no need for both of ye to leave here."

He ignored her, facing Eoghanan. "I canna imagine yer reasons for convincing her to do this, but I'll be damned if I let ye take her there. I doona trust ye, especially no with the women I love."

He expected his brother to react angrily, to show some form of self-defense. He'd not directly addressed Eoghanan in months. Instead, the look of pain in his brother's eyes made him feel guilty for his hasty words. Baodan knew he placed more blame on Eoghanan than was fair but, try as he might, he couldn't stop the resentment he felt toward him.

"I'm sorry that ye doona trust me, brother, for there is no one in the world that I trust more than ye. If ye wish to accompany Mother, then I shall remain here with Niall, but doona ever again suggest that I would harm her. No matter what ye blame me for, surely ye know I wouldna do that."

Baodan cast his eyes downward, ashamed and guilty. "Aye, o' course ye wouldna. Still, I will be the one to see her safely to the Camerons."

Eoghanan stood, speaking with his back toward the rest of the table as he exited the room. "As ye wish. I'm retiring for the evening. I'll come down in the morning to bid ye both farewell before ye leave."

Once Eoghanan left, Baodan faced Niall whose dark hair hung loosely in his face, covering his dark eyes. He knew Niall expected what he meant to ask him. "Can I count on ye to stay here and run things while I am away? To keep an eye on Eoghanan?"

"Aye, ye know that I will."

"There is no need for ye to watch Eoghanan. Ye have punished him for too long." His mother's words shocked him nearly as much as her sudden decision to leave their home.

He wouldn't allow himself to speak angrily to her, but he couldn't sit there while she defended him. "Why doona ye go up to yer bedchamber? I will send someone to help ye gather yer belongings. I need to be out of doors."

Not giving her a chance to respond, Baodan moved quickly from the room. It was a beautiful night, and he wished to sit out by the pond, to stare in it with hopes that its rippling surface would help some of his bitterness drift away.

* * *

Baodan kicked off his boots as he reached the water's edge, grinning as one of the leather footings splashed into the water. Perhaps, part of him had kicked it into the water on purpose. It was a pleasant summer evening, hot for Scotland. Although it was never good to have a wet shoe, it gave him the perfect excuse to go for a swim.

He glanced around to ensure that he wouldn't be revealing himself to any castle maids or female servants and, finding the pond and surrounding area empty, swiftly stripped down and dove into the chilly water.

The water proved a balm to his skin and soul, instantly relieving his flustered spirit and angry mind. He reached the shoe quickly, throwing it onto the shore to begin the slow process of drying before diving beneath the water's surface once more.

He swam as if racing, moving his arms in and out of the water, bobbing his head up and down as fast as he could manage. With each gasp of breath he pushed himself harder, each stroke of his arms helping to push away his worries and resentment of things past and present. He was in his element, his favorite place in the world, and only when his fingers and toes were wrinkled and freezing from being too long in the water did he feel most at peace in the world.

He found it now, as all worries washed away with each stroke. Dreamlike described the joy he felt as he pushed himself forward in the water, eyes closed to what lay before him.

The dream ended abruptly as he kicked himself forward and the corner of a rock tore its way into his flesh. He knew the pond well, but he'd gotten carried away, forgetting all about the patch of rocks that lay beneath the surface of the pond's center.

He knew it bled, the sting of the water's touch told him that much. Breathing between gritted teeth, he stroked his way back to the shore, crawling out onto the grass to check his injured foot. It wasn't a bad cut and would heal quickly although it would be sore for at least a few days.

Baodan leaned back onto his elbows and stared out across the black pond, only lit by the full moon hanging high above him. He was a good swimmer. Good thing too. If he hadn't been, it was likely that Blaire Conall would have drowned the

14

day he found her unconscious in the freezing ocean only a little over a year ago.

Thoughts of that day drifted away as he laughed softly to himself, thinking of his throbbing foot. His life seemed to be much like his unexpected cut. The times when things seemed most peaceful everything usually fell apart.

It happened with his late wife, although only his family knew what had truly happened to her. Everyone else believed she'd fallen ill, taken quickly by a fast progressing illness. In Baodan's mind, it wasn't all that far from the truth.

They'd only just married, and he thought himself so in love with her that she occupied his every thought, but he couldn't help but see the change in her shortly after they married. She grew dark and unhappy, miserable. She stopped speaking to him, and would hardly leave her bed. She waged battles within herself, and he knew of no way to help her.

During one of her darkest spells, he was forced to leave for a fortnight to help a man acquire a piece of land. He left her in Eoghanan's care, and his brother swore to watch after her.

The night he returned to the castle, Baodan found her hanging out one of the castle windows. Eoghanan claimed to have fallen so ill he couldn't move from his bed only hours before she killed herself.

Baodan lived with the guilt of not being able to save her always. He would not have let a sickness keep him from protecting her from the wickedness that invaded her mind.

Years later, the same had happened with his father's death. Life had just begun to take on some sense of normalcy when the sudden death of his father sent him spiraling downward once again. Optimistic Baodan released himself of

15

the hope of having the life he once dreamed of.

He did his best to remain kind, not to harden his heart against all of humanity, and in that he succeeded. He still found joy in his family, in running their home and land and people, still offered a helping hand when needed, but that was all the joy he allowed himself to feel. He took pleasure in the joy, security, and friendship he could bring to others but closed his heart from feeling all of that which others could bring to him. His hope had been broken too many times for him to allow it to creep back into his soul ever again.

He thought he found a person of similar mind and spirit in Blaire Conall. She was Blaire MacChristy when he rescued her from the freezing water, and the hurt in her eyes was enough to break his own heart. She was broken, defeated, and a reflection of what he'd been years ago. He wanted nothing more than to help her, to heal her heart with friendship rather than love.

For that reason, he proposed to her. Love was a horrible misery, one that he never intended to fall prey to ever again. He suspected that Blaire felt much the same way and, for two people who didn't want love, perhaps friendship was best.

She accepted his proposal, and he found himself happy that he would spend the rest of his days with someone whom he could share mutual companionship and respect, free of heartbreak or hope.

In what seemed to be a pattern in his life, his newest, smaller dream ended as well. Hope still flickered within Blaire, and she was far luckier than him. Her heartbreak was healed when her love, Arran Conall, came back to her, suddenly free from the confines of his own marriage.

Baodan let her go willingly. He couldn't begrudge her happiness if she could find it. If he were less broken, less hard and more lucky, he would gladly leap in the direction of love as Blaire had done.

Friendship was really all he'd offered her; friendship could remain although she was married to another, and so it had. He considered her to be his closest friend, a confidant when he had few. They wrote to each other often and, because she was married to his cousin, both families used the other's home as a stopping point when traveling. It became a happy friendship and one of the things in his life he was most grateful for.

Thinking of Blaire, he stood. Keeping his left foot off of the ground he tried to shake away the remaining water from his body and feelings of self-pity from his mind before donning his clothing so that he could go inside.

He had much to be thankful for. He could almost hear Blaire's voice telling him to quit his sulking and get on. His life would be what he made it, and he would fill it with kindness, friendship, and a pleasing lack of love.

* * *

Eoghanan glanced up from his writing desk to see his eldest brother staring into the pond outside his window. Baodan's tall frame and broad shoulders intimidated everyone at first glance, but his brother had the kindest of hearts, and the bitterness Eoghanan knew Baodan held toward him didn't suit his kind demeanor. If only Baodan knew the truth, perhaps years of pain would finally come to the end. For years he'd gladly carried his sister-in-law's secret, but he could do so no longer.

He suspected it even on the night of her death, but not until their mother fell ill did he realize the whole truth of what occurred that tragic night. No illness prevented him from protecting her, but a poison. And now his mother exhibited the very same symptoms.

Baodan was too blinded by his need to lay blame for his wife's downward spiral and tragic death to see the truth, but soon Eoghanan would have the proof he needed. Osla had not taken her own life that dark night so many years ago. Someone within the castle killed her, the same person who poisoned him to prevent him from saving her, and the same person who slowly poisoned their mother now.

All he needed to do was ensure his mother's safety.

To gather proof of the unthinkable.

Niall's secrets wouldn't keep for long.

Chapter 3

As anticipated, sleep eluded me. I spent the night tossing and turning, glancing at the clock every five minutes hoping that it was nearly sunrise so that I could get up and start my day.

I was ready for it to be three o'clock so that I could get the hell out of this house, this state. Every inch of the city, a memory I'd just rather forget. When it was finally six a.m., I jumped out of bed, put on my workout clothes, and left for a good long run.

I ran without direction, hoping that it would clear my head and exhaust me enough that I would, at the very least, be able to sleep on the plane. I enjoyed running and ran as fast as my feet would carry me, logging at least six miles before I rounded the block leading back to the house.

I stripped just inside the doorway of the house, anxious to get into a steaming hot shower. I showered in the guest bedroom, hoping that Brian and Leah had confined their activities to the master bedroom. It was a good thing Bri didn't seem to have any intention of coming back here. I was sure she would want to burn every last sheet, wash cloth, blanket, and towel. I wanted to do the same myself but knew, with my luck, I would probably end up burning the entire house to the ground.

Sufficiently pink and warm from the hot water, I dressed

in comfortable sweats for the plane and went about the business of packing the few items I thought necessary to bring. I didn't have much here. Most of my belongings were in storage, and I didn't want to go and collect them just for a trip.

Packed and ready to go by ten and not wanting to stay in the house a moment longer, I decided to go ahead and make my way to the airport. I didn't want to pay for parking, especially considering I wasn't sure how long I would be gone, so I called a taxi. It would be about a half hour wait before a driver could arrive, so I picked up my mess, locked up the house, and went to sit out on the front porch to wait for the cab.

It wasn't surprising, but still seemed quite odd to me that Bri would leave me an entire house. I always thought that was something people only did after they died and, thank God, she hadn't. I couldn't make myself stay in the house, so once I found Bri I intended to try and talk her into taking it back. If she wouldn't, I would simply sell it and use the money to re-stock my savings that had been painfully depleted due to the divorce.

The taxi driver arrived right on time, and I found myself at the airport, checked in and through security by noon. With three hours to kill, I decided to grab some lunch and maybe a drink, or two, or three, in the chain restaurant and bar located just down from my gate.

Eating alone is a strange thing. As I sat there munching on my plate of potato skins and sipping on a gargantuan margarita, I realized quite pathetically that I didn't ever remember doing this before. How does someone make it to the age of twenty-eight without ever having eaten in a restaurant all alone?

I knew the answer, but it made me utterly ashamed of my lack of independence. Of all the things in the world, I was most terrified of being alone; just another of the reasons I'd allowed myself to so easily fall under Brian's spell although I knew I didn't love him. Jep Franks was the only man I'd truly ever loved and, if I was honest, still loved. I married another simply because I couldn't stand the thought of being alone and didn't expect love like that to find its way to me ever again.

Sitting there alone, staring at couples and groups of people come in and out of the restaurant, I thought of Bri and how opposite of me she truly was. It was a wonder that we ever became such good friends. She would revel in the aloneness, the happy solitude of sitting by herself watching others' lives move around her. It made me feel alone and sad, wondering if others judged me for traveling alone. Did they think I was simply a runaway with no one to come along for the ride?

I always gave her such a hard time for spending so much time alone, but truth was, I envied her. Although she always had her lively yet flighty mother, she'd grown up just as alone as I. Instead of it making her dependent upon social interaction, she'd become strong and independent.

I'm not saying that I admired everything about Bri. Good grief, it was frustrating trying to get her to go out on a date. Men fawned over her, and she just simply never saw it. She was constantly oblivious to the glances and gawking eyes. Usually, I did the gawking. If I hadn't always been tied to a man, I would've taken advantage of my singleness. While I did wish to follow Bri's lead on the independence front, I had no intention of ending my gawking days.

The male species, the exception being Brian of course,

was made to be admired and now that I had been released from the prison of being married to the dark, cloudy, negative force Brian became, I intended to do a lot of admiring.

* * *

With a fresh perspective and a much more upbeat attitude, part of which could be attributed to finishing off that second margarita, I paid my bill and went to freshen up a bit in the bathroom before finding a seat at my gate so that I could await boarding.

Although I wore sweats, I made an effort this morning, feeling the need to look as pretty as possible in the hopes that it would lift my spirits. That, and the aforesaid margaritas, seemed to do the trick, pleasing me with what I saw in the mirror. Apparently though, the woman standing next to me didn't agree.

I saw her out of the corner of my eye, in skin tight cheetah print pants, high heels, and a deep v-cut that I couldn't have pulled off in my wildest dreams. She busied herself by applying at least half a case of blush onto her already blushed cheeks. The oddest part of her ensemble were the cowboy boots that went halfway up her calf and the bright blue cowboy hat that balanced perilously on top of her rolling carry-on. She very much resembled a drag-queen that I saw once in a Las Vegas show, with the top of her hair pulled into a poof at least three inches high. I wasn't altogether sure that she wasn't and found myself glancing in between her legs in the mirror to see if the she/he had a special package tucked up and away.

I could tell nothing, the fabric too busy to reveal anything. I turned away to grab some paper towels before exiting the bathroom. I knew I should've felt guilty, or at the very least ashamed for staring at the woman's crotch, but alcohol had blurred the edges slightly of what I felt appropriate. Then again, what did she expect from dressing that way?

I'd just finished drying my hands when her voice behind me caused me to jump out of my skin. Exceedingly female, very fake, and drenched in a thick Texas accent, I smiled at the wall. He was definitely a woman minus the "wo." I'd lived in Texas all my life and had only heard a Texas accent that pronounced in the movies.

"Wait just a minute, sugar. I'd like to offer you some assistance."

I spun slowly, my brows knitted together in confusion. "Assistance? I wasn't aware that I needed any." The words came out a little sharp, but I really felt that second drink and the little filter I had left the building.

The she/he, I wasn't sure how to think of him, reared back with wide eyes. "Oh, what a feisty thing you are, but yes, you do need assistance. You are far too gorgeous for me to let you go back out there like that. You have the darkest circles under your eyes, you look as if you haven't slept in days."

I remained facing the same direction but cast a sideways glance into the mirror. Although I hadn't noticed it before, deep, dark circles shaded the skin beneath my eyes. Not that it was any wonder, I suffered from sleep deprivation. "I'm afraid you're right, but there's not much I can do about it. My makeup is in my checked bag."

She/he smiled wide and reached down to grab a bag sitting next to the rolling carry-on. "Not to worry, sugar, I've got just the thing."

Before I could protest, the stranger unwrapped a fresh sponge and slathered violet-colored cream underneath my eyes. I glanced down to see a boarding pass hanging out of the bag. I smiled, my suspicion completely confirmed. "Umm...Tom, I appreciate your help, but can I ask you what you're doing in the women's restroom?"

His hand froze on my face, and he instantly lost the female voice and Texas accent as he grinned guiltily. "Dammit. I should've zipped that up. Okay, don't freak out, I'm not some weirdo. I'm an actor on my way to L.A. to audition for a movie. I have to go straight from the plane to the audition so I had to go ahead and get in character. I couldn't very well go into the men's restroom looking like this. There. See?" He stepped away so that I could turn to examine his work.

I looked much better, certainly more awake and sober than I felt. "Thank you. I don't easily freak out." What was I saying? I definitely did freak out easily, but I felt especially chill. "Let me guess, the part you're auditioning for...drag queen?"

He laughed hard, and the deep voice sounded extremely odd coming from the female-ish face. "One would think, but no actually. Well, not exactly. Think *Mrs. Doubtfire*, except more cops and less children, and.." he hesitated and reached up to scratch his head. "Actually, it's nothing like that."

I grinned and laughed. "Alright, well that sounds just great. I do look much better. I appreciate it. Let me return the favor." Before he could respond, I turned to grab another paper towel, wetting it beneath the running faucet. Wringing it out, I reached up to dab it over his cheeks, rinsing away some of the excess blush. "Don't take offense, but it seems that you're much better at doing someone else's make-up than your own."

"None taken. All this is new to me. All you needed was a

little light under your eyes which was simple. This…" he circled his face with his fingers. "This is a little harder for me to deal with."

Satisfied, I pulled away and chunked the paper towel into the trash can. I glanced at my watch and quickly reached down to grab my bag. "Oh gracious, I've got to go. Almost time to board. Thanks again for your help, and good luck at your audition."

"My pleasure. Try and get some sleep on the plane. You seem to be in need of it." He surprised me by reaching behind me before I could leave, quickly grabbing the clip that held my hair into a messy bun at the base of my neck. His eyes widened as my long, red curls cascaded over my shoulders and down my back.

"That's better. Why the hell would you pin all that up?"

I reached up fluffing the hair into place as I tucked it behind my ears. "It's easier that way. I'm traveling, who's going to see it?"

He shook his head in disbelief. "Everybody in the airport is going to notice you, sweetie, whether your hair is pulled up or not. Besides, that is some killer hair. I wish I'd been able to find a wig like that." With that, he turned and left me in the bathroom.

After taking a second to laugh at the odd occurrence, I snatched up my bag and made haste to my gate. When I got there, they were already lining up to board. I was in the first group and, taking my place in the back of the line, I waited my turn for my ticket to be scanned. Smiling at the attendant as she tore my pass, I stepped out onto the walkway leading to the plane.

Amazing, the difference a few hours could make. This

morning things seemed bleak, but now I felt more excited than I'd been in ages. This trip could be great and, for the first time in the five years since I'd met Brian, I was finally free.

Chapter 4

He should still been sleeping. A long journey lay ahead of him once he left with his mother for Cameron Castle, but he wanted to speak with Eoghanan alone before his mother woke.

Eoghanan would be awake. He wasn't sure if his mysterious brother ever slept. He would be in his room, writing away by candlelight in his journals. What he wrote, Baodan was sure he would never know. Not that he cared. It took all his strength just to remain civil around him.

As expected, Baodan found his brother hunched over his writing desk, scribbling away, his shoulders stiff and uncomfortable looking. He didn't look up as Baodan entered. Instead of announcing his presence, Baodan walked across the room, only stopping once he stood next to his brother's desk. He glanced down at the secretive pages, but Eoghanan yanked them away, breaking his rigid stance by standing abruptly.

"These are not for ye to look at. If I wished ye to see them, I would have addressed them to ye, aye?" Eoghanan's eyes green, gold, and cat-like challenged him as he widened his stance. His unruly red hair, like dancing flames atop his head.

Baodan stepped away, not wishing things to escalate. He only wanted to find out the truth behind their mother's desire to leave, not to re-hash ill feelings. "I'm sorry, I dinna come here to spy on ye. I only wished to speak to ye before leaving."

Eoghanan looked suspicious. Baodan knew he'd given him more than enough reason to be. He'd spent every year since his wife's death trying to avoid speaking with his brother about anything.

"Why? Ye doona ever wish to speak to me."

Baodan reached up to run both hands through his hair and over his face. Eoghanan had once been his closest friend in the world. It seemed odd to him that he should feel so uncomfortable speaking to him now. "'Tis about Mother. I need to know why ye have convinced her to leave. Whether Aunt Nairne wishes to see her or no, Mother wouldna have come to the decision to leave on her own. I canna figure out why ye see the need for her to leave here. Do ye no wish to help care for her? No even while she is ill?"

"Aye, o' course I wish to care for her. Can ye no see 'tis for that reason that I insist she leave? I doona care what ye think of me. I love her just as much as ye do."

Why did he feel the need to be so vague? Baodan had no reason to assume that the change would be in their mother's best interest. "No, I canna see that her illness would be a reason for ye to make her leave here. I doona doubt that ye care for her, but ye are no telling the truth of what ye mean by all of this."

"No, and I willna tell ye all there is to it either. 'Tis no me place to do so. No yet."

Baodan moved across the room so that Eoghanan would not see his frustration, but the tone of his voice gave it away. "Is that so? I doona believe it was yer place to allow me wife to die, but ye did so any way. Why worry about what is and isna yer place now?"

In a rare show of anger his brother charged him,

slamming him up against the wall.

"Ye are an ignorant fool. Do ye think that speaking to me in such a way will make me inclined to tell ye why Mother must leave? I willna tell ye anything of it for ye wouldna hear me even if I did. Ye have closed yerself off to me, and ye have punished me long enough. She has been gone for over seven years, Baodan. Do ye truly believe that I wouldna have helped her if I'd been able?"

Baodan could hardly speak as shock coursed through him. Eoghanan released him and stepped away shaking, pain evident in his voice and his eyes watery with anguish. Baodan moved away from the wall, eager to leave.

Eoghanan brought out the worst in him. He hated the person he'd become around his youngest brother. The very reason he spent so much time avoiding him.

"I'll bid ye goodbye now, brother. I only wished to learn why she must leave, but I can see that I willna gain the information from ye. I canna believe ye have coerced Mother into doing this. She's so ill she can hardly lift spoon to mouth. We will be lucky if she survives the trip."

Baodan moved toward the door, only stopping at the sound of his brother's voice, soft, small, and so different from how he sounded a moment before. A voice filled with warning rather than anger.

"She willna only survive the trip, she shall thrive from it. Just wait and see how her health improves once she is away from this castle. Then perhaps ye will see that I wasna wrong to persuade her to leave."

Baodan left quickly, more frustrated than he'd been before entering his brother's room. Why had his life become a series of riddles in which everyone around him seemed to know the answers, save him? Something hid from him. If he could get through the next few days without any more surprises, he intended to devote his every effort to finding out what that was.

* * *

He wished to make one more stop before he left to prepare the horses. If his mother still rested when all was ready, he would wait until she elected to leave. She would need all the strength she could muster for the several days trip. He would not be the one to disturb her.

Baodan rounded the corner and knocked on Niall's bedchamber door. Niall wouldn't be awake like Eoghanan, and Baodan found himself hesitant to enter his brother's room unannounced. Quite likely there would be a lass with him, and Baodan would rather not embarrass the girl unlucky enough to be in his bed.

Niall was a charmer, but Baodan knew him, and he knew what a liar he was as well. Each woman that shared his chamber entered due to his exclamations of love and promises. In exchange for a night in his arms, each lass would find herself heartbroken and quickly forgotten in turn.

When no response came, Baodan rapped his fist against the doorway louder, stepping away as he heard his brother's grumbling voice through the doorway.

"What the hell do ye want? Can ye no see that the sun is still no up? I doona rise until it does."

Baodan stared at the door, annoyed. Everyone in the castle knew the sun to be near midday before Niall chose to rise from his bed. When the door finally swung open, Niall stood before him nude, his hair sticking up messily as his black eyes stared up at Baodan. He expected Niall's grumpy reaction and stared down at his brother who stood a great deal shorter than him, waiting his response.

"Would ye like to have yer nose knocked up into yer skull, brother? I have company and was having the sweetest dreams."

Baodan shook his head, not the least bit surprised. "Ye shouldna treat women so. They are no created for ye to enjoy and toss aside."

Niall laughed, and Baodan reached around his brother to close the bedchamber door so that the lass sleeping in the bed would not hear their conversation.

"Ye are a fool if ye truly believe that, Baodan. 'Tis the only reason they exist as far as I'm concerned."

Baodan chuckled once, throwing his hands up in surrender. "Then I suppose I am a fool, for I doona agree with ye. 'Tis a twisted way to look at any lass, but I know there are many men who think as ye do so I willna fault ye for it. I only wish that ye wouldna tease them so with yer sweet words and false promises."

"I doona wish to be with the lasses who wouldna care if I made me true feelings known. They doona care for themselves like lassies truly looking for love. Now," Niall crossed his arms, clearly not pleased with being lectured, "did ye come here to make me feel guilty or did ye have something different that ye wished to say to me?"

"Aye, I wished to see if ye know why Eoghanan would want Mother to leave here. I canna see any sense to it. I thought perhaps ye might be able to help me see a reason for this." The look on Niall's face made him regret his decision to speak to him. Niall's relationship with their mother had always been strained.

"No, I doona know what to tell ye for I doona know and I doona care. I shall no be sad to see her go."

Baodan's jaw tightened at Niall's words. "Ye should be ashamed of yerself for saying such a thing."

"Why? She doesna like me, and she makes it clear."

The look of disgust on Niall's face made Baodan's fists clench together in anger. He turned away, knowing his temper was about to flare. He didn't look back as he walked away, only speaking loudly so that Niall could hear him. "Perhaps 'tis the way ye treat women and the way ye lie to everyone around ye that makes her no so fond of ye. I canna say I like ye much meself at the moment. Watch over the keep while I am away."

Fuming, Baodan exited the castle's main entrance as fast as he could. He shuddered at the thought of Niall's thoughtless words. It made him wonder just how good of a man he could be when both his brothers were the worst sort of men.

Chapter 5

On The Plane To Scotland

Present Day

I was drooling. So much for looking attractive. With my head slumped against the window of the plane and cold drool dribbling out the side my mouth, attractive was the last word anyone would use to describe me. I fell asleep just as soon as I settled into my seat, and as the unpleasant tickle woke me, I realized I wasn't sure if we were in the air yet.

Eyes still closed, I raised my head off the side of the window and ran the back of my hand over my chin and mouth. With no turbulence or movement as far as I could tell, I assumed that we'd yet to take off. Planning on resuming my slumber within seconds, I reluctantly opened my eyes and slid the plastic cover on the window up just slightly so that I could peek outside.

Sure enough, I saw tarmac rather than sky, and it was clear there had been some sort of delay. I groaned and started to close the window when a familiar voice to my left caused my hand to freeze on the shade.

"Hey there, sleepy. I almost woke you, but you looked like you really needed some shuteye. I couldn't believe it when I got to my seat and saw you sitting there. What's it been, Mits, five years? Surely we will take off soon. We've been sitting here for over an hour."

I didn't turn, didn't even respond as I sat there pinching my eyes closed while facing the window of the plane. I quickly tried to think back to the restaurant. Had I really only drank two margaritas? The incident in the bathroom had been weird enough, but this? This was just too much. The chances of this happening were so small, I sincerely couldn't believe it was really Jep's voice I heard behind me.

"Mits? Are you okay?"

If only I didn't need to pee so badly, perhaps I could simply lay my head down and feign sleep for the duration of the flight. Unfortunately, I did have to go to the bathroom. I'd gone into the restroom inside the airport and never ended up inside a stall. Besides, it might have been five years since I'd seen him, but I still knew Jep well enough to know that he wouldn't let me deplane without speaking to him. And why would he? He'd been my best friend, and I his, for over twelve years.

We'd been childhood friends and then young lovers, and he'd smashed my heart into a gazillion pieces.

Knowing I couldn't face this direction forever and, with the length in between us speaking growing awkwardly long, I swallowed the lump that formed in the middle of my chest at hearing his voice and faced him.

I smiled as I looked him over, hoping he would be unable to see every thought that ran through my mind. He'd changed. His previously dirty blonde hair was darker, and his brown eyes were tired, less hopeful than they'd once been. Small bags pouched his eyes, the kind that men get as they grow older, but he was too young to have them already. He seemed to have aged too quickly in the few short years since I'd seen him last.

I glanced down at his left hand to find he was still married. If his marriage even remotely resembled what mine had been, it went a long way toward explaining why he looked so much older.

If he was a stranger and I was meeting him for the first time, I don't think I would have found him overly attractive, but he wasn't a stranger and, despite the changes in him, I found him just as handsome as always.

I swallowed once more and said a silent prayer in the hopes that my voice wouldn't come out shaky and weird. "Jep! I've never been so surprised to see anyone. Why are you going to Scotland?"

He smiled back and reached across the armrest to pull me toward him. "Business. Now come here. It's been too long since I've held you in my arms."

He wrapped his arms around me and held me close, but I immediately felt uncomfortable. What an odd thing for him to say. A sentiment I spent a lot of my time thinking, but never one that I expected him to return. While I found myself thinking of him often, I knew there was no reason for me to ever cross his mind.

He could sense how rigid I became in his embrace and released it quickly, pulling one half of his mouth up into a quirky grin while glancing down at the floor. "I'm sorry. That was weird of me to say. It's just…"

A ding above us interrupted his apology as the captain came over the speakers to tell us that the problem had been fixed and we would be cleared for takeoff shortly. Once the plane started moving, I would be unable to go to the bathroom until after we were in the air a good ways. I couldn't wait that long.

Unbuckling, I stood to make my way to the lavatory. "Sorry, I'll be right back. I've got to go before the plane takes off."

He nodded and I made my exit, taking a deep breath for the first time since I'd heard his voice. I couldn't imagine what he would say, but I was sure I didn't want to hear it. Any re-hashing of memories would only make me ache, and I'd just set my mind to being much more positive only an hour ago.

His words of goodbye the last time I saw him, while kinder, were more hurtful to me than anything Brian could ever say. I cared about Jep that much more.

After relieving myself, I dreadfully made my way back to my seat. The nearness of him made everything inside me hum. When we'd been together, my body hummed much the same way but it was with excitement, anticipation, love; now, the humming was different, caused by palpable tension and unsaid words. It wasn't angry tension by any means, but the tension that is always shared by two people who have a shared history and un-shared feelings.

As soon as I sat down, the plane moved and, for the duration of the takeoff, both of us remained silent. After we were in the air and the atmosphere in the cabin changed back to one where people visited quietly, while others slept or read, I could see Jep's hands start to twitch nervously. I knew he was about to say something.

I closed my eyes to try the tactic I'd thought of earlier but, as anticipated, it didn't work.

Finally gathering his nerves, Jep reached out to squeeze my hand gently before pulling it away as my eyes opened.

"I know you're not asleep. Can I ask you something?"

I didn't respond immediately, instead trying to weigh the chances of him actually refraining from asking the question if I told him no. The chances weren't very good. "Um…sure." I said it slowly, on purpose. I wanted him to know that I was reluctant to chat.

"Where did you go?"

"What?"

He shifted in his seat so that he faced me. "After the wedding? Where did you go?"

It seemed rude to stare straight ahead while he studied me so intensely, so I matched his stare. "I didn't go anywhere. Brian and I stayed in Austin. I got a job as a teacher's aide at a local elementary school. Why do you ask?"

He looked down again. I'd never seen him so hesitant about anything. He was usually over-confident, even leaning on the side of cocky. "That's not what I meant, but I'm surprised to know that you didn't leave Austin, and we've never bumped into each other. I don't see a ring on your finger. Are you and Brian? Are you still?"

I was tired, cranky and, if he insisted on talking, I wished he would just say whatever it was he meant to. "No, we're not. Look, I don't want to be rude, but I'm exhausted and, even once we land, I have a several hours car drive ahead of me. Just spit out whatever it is you're talking about. What do you mean, that's not what you meant?"

His eyes swept downward, and it did nothing to help me sympathize with him. "I mean, I didn't hear from you anymore after my wedding."

I was older, both in age and in life experience since my time with Jep, and I wouldn't allow him to make me feel guilty over something that was his fault ever again. "What?" I spoke loudly enough to garner attention from people around us so I lowered my voice and leaned in slightly closer to him. "Did you honestly expect to? You married her! I know we'd been broken up a while, but we talked every day, all the time, and you got engaged and married, all without telling me! Surely, after all of the years we've known each other, you knew I wasn't going to call and text a married man?"

He looked up from the floor and locked eyes with me. "I did know, and I couldn't stand the thought of not talking to you. That's why I didn't tell you until after the fact."

"It was a selfish thing to do. And don't tell me that you couldn't stand the thought of not talking to me. The things you said to me after your wedding were meant to guarantee that you would never hear from me ever again." I stopped speaking before my voice could crack. Thinking back on the night I learned he'd married was enough to take all the breath out of me.

Jep reached his hand up and caressed the side of my face. I almost pulled away, but the touch was comforting and I chose to lean into it.

"I was lying. I was sure you would know. It was self-preservation, preservation for my marriage. I had to push you away, but I always thought you would know. Surely you do. I always loved you. I did back then, and I do now. I'm not sure that you ever truly stop loving anyone once you've fallen in love with them."

He dropped his hand, and I twisted in my seat toward the front once more. I breathed deeply, thinking on what he'd said. Hearing those words was like being released from a set of chains I didn't consciously even know I wore.

In that moment I realized it wasn't so much the loss of Jep that wounded me so much all those years ago, but the loss of love. For me to have known how much I loved him and to hear him say that he'd never loved me, despite all the years we'd spent together, was more painful than him moving on to someone else. If I'd at least known that my love had been reciprocated, it would have been easier to move on.

Sleepy, I closed my eyes before speaking to him again. "It doesn't change anything you know. You were an important part of my life, but it wasn't ever supposed to be me and you, in the end."

His voice was quiet, but I could hear the same relief in his voice that I felt in my soul. "I know, but I needed to tell you."

I smiled, eyes still closed as I spoke through a large yawn. "I know, and that's all I ever needed to hear."

Why then with this settled and Brian out of my life did I feel the future would demand more than my past ever had?

Chapter 6

"Why do ye look so pleased with yerself, love? Yer cheeks are sure to be sore if ye go on grinning like that."

Morna Conall stepped inside the doorway of their charming home to plant a sound kiss upon her husband who stood waiting for her in the entryway. Grayed-hair framed his wrinkled face, but his thin mouth smiled against hers as she kissed him. His plaid blue shirt, wrinkled, hung loosely on his slim frame, and the smell of pipe tobacco lingered near him. No matter that his knees creaked and his ears required that she speak up, he would remain ageless in her eyes always.

"I doona know what ye mean, Jerry. I'm just pleased that Mitsy arrives today. 'Tis good to feel useful once more, and I'm anxious to see how the spell works now that I've tweaked it." She knew her husband would know she wasn't being completely honest, but she found Jerry charming when he was all riled up.

"Aye, but that isna why ye are grinning so. If I know ye as well as I think I do, and believe me I do, then I would say that ye've already been making yerself useful and using yer spells a bit, aye? Now, what is it that ye have done?"

Stepping out of her shoes, Morna moved into the living room and sat on the couch, patting the seat next to her so that Jerry would join her. She reached to brush the red hair that turned whiter with each passing year out of her face. With

Jerry seated, she reached for his hands and spoke. "All I did was re-arrange a flight ticket so that a certain lad would be on board with her."

"Why would ye do that? What is the purpose of her coming here if the man she's supposed to meet resides in the States?"

Jerry's voice came out high and confused, and Morna laughed as she squeezed the old man's hand. "The lad she's meant for isna in the States. I only wished to learn what occurred in her past that led her to us. So I did some casting to find it. Ye see, there's always much more to the end of a marriage than the actual end of it."

If only all relationships were lucky enough to be matched by her, Morna was certain there'd be many less hurting hearts in the world. She was a master at it, and she believed that to provide aide in the creation of love was the best use of her magic.

"Aye, that there is, dear. Did ye put Mitsy's husband on the plane?"

Morna shook her head. "Ex-husband now, and o' course I dinna! In Mitsy's case, her deepest wound was no from her marriage but from someone that came before it. She needed that wound to be healed before she goes back in time. I believe allowing them both the chance to speak to one another did just that."

"Now, why is that, love? Why did she need to be rid of her hurt? Hurt is something that we all must learn from, and time heals our hurts well enough on its own."

Morna smiled. She found her husband to be wiser for his lack of magic. "Perhaps ye are right about time but, in this case, I thought time needed a little help."

41

"And just why is that? Ye are goading me by finishing every sentence without giving a full explanation, and I doona like it."

Morna laughed as her husband's voice rose at the end of his question. He quickly grew frustrated. She kissed him swiftly on the cheek and leaned into him as she spoke. "Aye, I know that I am but I canna help it, ye make it too much fun."

He glared back at her, only causing her to laugh more.

"Fine, fine. I'm finished. I just believe that now that Mitsy is free of feelings that were holding her back, she will be free to help someone who will need her assistance to free himself."

A sudden knock on the door caused them both to jerk their heads toward the entranceway.

Jerry stood, moving slowly toward the foyer. "How did ye no see that she was about to be here?"

Morna moved to join her husband. "The casting distracted me. I was eager to see the results of my efforts with the plane tickets. Not to mention,"

"The fact that ye will have to lie to the lass," Jerry's voice finished her sentence and Morna looked down regretfully. "Aye, we shall both have to. 'Tis the only way to get the lass where she truly needs to be, and that place isna with Bri at Conall Castle."

* * *

Jep and I both left the plane as quite different people than those who boarded it. With the mutual feeling that the past was truly behind both of us, we parted amicably and happily. It didn't take long to gather my luggage as I'd checked only one bag and, since this was my second time to rent a car to go in search of the odd innkeepers, the process went smoothly.

Several hours later, I found myself parked outside of the inn, anxious to get inside so that I could speak to Bri. If she wasn't inside the inn, I knew she had to be close.

Rather than the furious and frantic knock of my previous visit, I knocked softly now and stepped away from the door. The last time I arrived at the inn, I'd been in a bit of a panic and had not displayed the kindest manners.

It took a moment, but as soon as the door swung open, I was pulled into a surprisingly firm embrace.

"Ach, lass. I'm pleased that ye made it safely. Come inside, Mitsy. It's good to see ye, dear."

Once the elderly man released me, I tried to smile past the shock of the familiar greeting. "Thank you. It's good to see you...Jerry, is it?"

He beamed and patted me firmly on the shoulder, pulling my purse off my shoulder to set it beside the door in the process. "Aye, it was kind of ye to remember me name."

I stepped inside just a little bit further so that I could glance around for any sign of Bri or her husband, Eoin. "Yes, I remember your name, but I'm afraid I'm not sure of your wife's name. When I met her, she was Gwendolyn, but I heard Bri refer to her as Morna?"

As if summoned, Jerry's wife stepped into the entranceway and embraced me much the same way as Jerry had done. "Call me Morna, dear. And ye did remember me names, both of them. 'Tis only that ye dinna remember which one to use."

Friendly folks I thought to myself, but truthfully, I didn't mind the affection at all, I was merely surprised by it, especially considering how terribly I'd treated them both upon my first visit here. "I'm afraid I owe both of you an apology. The first time I came here, well, I was very rude. I was only - - " I was interrupted by Morna who spoke as she waved me inside the kitchen.

"No need to apologize. You were worried about Bri. It only goes to show what a good friend ye are. Come, sit and eat a bit. I've made chicken pot pie. Not a Scottish dish, to be sure, but when me American friends come to visit, I like to try American recipes."

Jerry wrinkled up his nose, and I laughed at the disgust on his face.

"Aye, well at least ye dinna make the lasagna this time."

Morna ignored him. As soon as I was seated, I dug into the delicious dish. "It's wonderful. Thank you. Might I ask you a question?"

Morna sat down across from me and Jerry followed, sitting next to her. "O'course ye can. I suppose ye are anxious to know how things are to happen now?"

I frowned but stared down at my food so as not to show my utter confusion. "I just wanted to ask you if Bri was here?"

The pitch of Morna's voice caused me to look up. She seemed as shocked as I was confused. "Well, o'course she isna here, dear. She told ye where she was, dinna she?"

Was everyone around here smoking the same thing? Surely, she didn't believe that Bri was living in the seventeenth century? "Well, she did tell me something, but come on? It was obviously some sort of weird joke. I don't know why she wouldn't tell me the truth."

Morna stood and moved to a coat closet out in the hallway from the kitchen. When she returned, she extended a plain, brown dress and a smooth, black rock in my direction. It looked like something you would put on at a carnival to take an old-timey photo. "She wasna lying to ye, Mitsy, and, if ye wish to see Bri, ye must go back as well."

I didn't say anything but just sat there, looking at them as if they were crazy. I half expected camera crews to pop out of the woodwork any moment to tell me I was on some sort of hidden camera show.

Jerry reached across the table and squeezed my hand in an effort to comfort me, but it only served to make me jump out of my seat.

"Okay, seriously, what the hell is going on? I really wanted to be nicer to you people this time, but you are freaking me out. Bri's had her fun, but I am really not in the mood. So tell her to get her skinny ass out here, or I am going to kick it so far she really does land in the seventeenth century."

The odd couple glanced uncomfortably at one another and then back in my direction. Morna finally spoke, "I canna make Bri come out here. I'm sorry, lass. I doona blame ye for thinking us mad. All of it seems so commonplace to me now, I forget that 'tis truly traumatic for those unaccustomed to the idea. I have magic, dear, a witch if ye like, and Bri truly is living in Conall Castle but in the year 1647. Ye willna believe it until ye are there, I'm sure. While it will be a rough adjustment, I can see that there willna be another way. Here's the long and short of it, Mitsy. If ye really wish to see Bri again, ye will step into the bathroom, change into the dress and do as we bid ye."

"Trust us," Jerry whispered softly.

*   *   *

Her eyes flashed when she ordered me into the bathroom and, while I believed Morna to be harmless, in that instant, if there were really such things as witches, she could have indeed been one.

I did as she asked, the whole while trying to figure out any plausible cause for what she was talking about. Perhaps it was a role-playing thing. That nerdy thing that video-game people do where they gather in fields and pretend to be things and people they're not, for fantasy-type battles. Surely, Bri wouldn't be involved in such a thing.

My next thought, and the only one that truly made any sense to me, was that it was some sort of creepy cult, something that Bri had gotten sucked into after she met Eoin, and they somehow managed to brainwash her so that she actually believed all this time-travel business. If it was a cult, I imagined the only way I would ever see Bri again was to play along and act as if I believed them so that they would bring me into their secret gathering place. I wasn't sure I could do it, but I could try. If it meant bringing Bri back into reality, I would do it whole-heartedly.

Once I stripped myself of the sweats I wore, I climbed into the dress, squirming against the hard package of something I could feel on the inside of the dress. I couldn't do up the laces myself, so hesitantly I stepped back into the kitchen.

"Look." I pointed a finger at both Morna and Jerry and put on my angriest "ginger" face. "This is obviously some sort of crazy-ass cult thing and, while I'll play along so that I get to see Bri, I don't want you to think for a moment that you're going to be able to brainwash me. You got it?"

Morna rolled her eyes dramatically, and Jerry started

laughing so hard he doubled over in the kitchen. It did nothing to calm me down.

"Believe what ye wish, lass, but in due time ye will see that ye are the one who is mad for dreaming up such a ridiculous notion." She paused to raise her palm in my direction. "But aye, lass, I swear not to try and brainwash ye."

I spun my back toward her. "Well, good. Just so it's clear. I'm only here for my friend and then we are both getting the hell out of here." I lowered my voice and spoke much more sweetly. I knew I sounded crazy, too. "Now, would you please help me with the laces? I couldn't do them on my own."

"Sure, dear."

Each time she pulled on the laces, the lump on the inside of the dress pushed into my side. "What's inside the dress? Is it some sort of tracking device? If so, I can assure you the dress is coming off as soon as I leave here."

With the next tug, I was certain she pulled on the lace a little tighter than was absolutely necessary. "Ye no doubt have a bit of Irish ancestry in ye, doona ye dear? For ye are as mad as a wee banshee. I sewed some ibuprofen and a few other medicines into the dress. Believe me, ye will need them once ye travel backward."

"Crazy as hell, every one of you," I muttered the words under my breath and was rewarded with a tug so tight, it knocked the air right out of me.

"What was that, dear?"

"Nothing." It came out weak and breathless. I should've kept that thought in my head.

Morna stepped away and motioned for Jerry and me to follow her. "Come along. It will take us several hours to get there. We best get on the road."

* * *

"I thought Bri was 'living' at Conall Castle?" I asked the question sarcastically. No one lived at Conall Castle, it had been a tourist attraction for many years and was no longer inhabited by anyone.

"Ye are going to Conall Castle, but ye must travel there by way of the pond at McMillan Castle. It has magical qualities."

"Of course it does." I stared at the window, enjoying the green beauty, despite being held hostage by two crazy bags. The landscape was so different from Texas, and in the best possible way.

We turned down a secluded gravel road, and I knew the instant we had reached our destination. The beauty of it took my breath way. A grand pond sat off to the right of the magnificent castle. It was smaller than Conall Castle but equally as exquisite. For a brief moment, I imagined being one of the ladies who'd been lucky enough to live there during its prime.

As quickly as the odd thought came, I rejected it. Lucky? They didn't have toilet paper, electricity, running water, or tampons. Oh, and let's not forget about birth control! Lucky was entirely the wrong word, but staring at the beauty of the place made it easy to romanticize the past in a way much more pleasant than I was certain it actually was.

Morna parked next to the pond and quickly got out of the car as she waved to me to follow. Seeing no choice but to do so, I did as she bid. Standing next to the water, I bent to dip my fingers into its surface. It was cold, but what was I expecting? It was Scotland, after all.

I turned to throw a frustrated look in Morna's direction. "Just how exactly is coming to the pond going to take me to Bri and the band of lunatics?"

"Ye must skip the rock, dear. If it skips three times, it shall take ye where ye need to go. Or, ye can hold it close to ye and float on yer back while we push ye into the water, but I suppose skipping it would be more fun for ye. If ye decide that ye need to come back, use the rock the same way."

I laughed and reared my arm back to chunk the rock, but waited as I asked Morna another question. "And just how do you expect me to do that? After I skip the rock, won't it disappear by floating to the bottom?"

She shook her head and laughed, clearly thinking my question stupid. "No, it will find its way right back to ye. Just like the pond is magical, so is the rock."

"Oh, right. How stupid of me." I faced the water once more. "Are you joining me, or am I jumping on the crazy train alone?"

Jerry patted me on the back and turned to head back to the car. "Good luck, dear, and good luck to whoever finds ye there first."

"Start the car, Jerry. I'll be there in a moment." Morna bent down to pick up a handful of smooth rocks. "No, we willna be joining ye. This is for ye to do alone. Now, why doona ye practice with these rocks first?"

I dismissed her hand. I'd taken many picnics and jogs around Lake Travis, and I knew how to skip a rock with the best of them.

"I don't need to practice." Rearing back, I flicked my wrist and watched the rock bounce. Once. Twice. I turned my head to Morna. "See, three times…"

49

In that instant, everything went black.

Chapter 7

McMillan Castle

1647

He wouldn't wake her, but Baodan hoped his mother would rise soon. He was anxious to leave here. His brothers put him in a bad mood indeed. If only all people were more like animals, perhaps he wouldn't have such a bad taste in his mouth for many of those nearest him. He ran his hands down the side of the marbled horse, leaning his head against the gentle beast.

"Ach, Artair, ye are a fine lad. What would ye say if we moved Niall and Eoghanan out here, and I moved ye and Heather into the castle? Ye could both have yer own bedchamber, and I wouldna mind if ye dined with me at the grand table."

The horse neighed happily and Baodan laughed as he tugged on both horses' reins, walking them out of the stables. "Aye, ye would both like that I expect, but alas, I was only teasing. I do care for them ye know, even Eoghanan. Despite how hard they make it, they're me brothers. Besides, I doona think Rhona would stand for it. She cleans up after the rest of us too much as 'tis."

A strange movement out of the corner of his eye caught his attention, and he whirled to face it. He was a good ways from the pond, but he could see something floundering in it. A bird, perhaps? He continued to move forward with the horses, straining his eyes to try and make out what tossed about in the water so frantically.

He heard it then, the faint scream so soft he thought perhaps he imagined it. There were no females around who would have gone for a swim. He turned to Artair "Did ye hear that, boy?"

The scream reached him once more, and the ears of both horses perked up as they took off at full speed in front of him. Baodan ran in the same direction. Although the horses stopped at the water's edge, Baodan dove into the chilly water as he reached it.

There was indeed a woman in the water, right at the water's center. He glanced up in between powerful strokes to see a lass with bountiful red hair bobbing up and down yelling angrily.

He slowed as he reached her. The lass wasn't drowning. She treaded water quite well, cursing with every other word.

She had the strangest accent, much like his cousin's wife, Bri. Although he didn't understand half of the words she shouted, he sensed none of them were appropriate to be coming out of a woman's mouth.

*   *   *

The impact of the water as I hit was unlike anything I'd experienced before. I imagined it to be something like diving off the high-dive without any form. I would be sore for days.

I couldn't explain it – what happened from the moment I threw the rock to the moment I hit the water. One minute I was on the shore, the next everything around me went black, the next, water rushed up into my nose as I sunk into the water.

Luckily, I reacted quickly, and I pushed my way up to the surface as soon as I registered that I was under water. I could swim well, although I preferred tip-toeing into the water to being catapulted into it.

My head was bleeding, I reached up to touch it as I treaded to get my bearings, and my hand came away covered in blood. It didn't hurt, but I suppose I was in some sort of shock from the sudden jolt. I wasn't altogether sure whether I hit my head upon immersing, or I'd been wacked over the head so that I could be tossed into it.

I spun in a circle and, for the first time, saw just how far I was from any shore. No way had I been thrown into the water. But if not, how else did I end up here? I started to scream. At Morna, at Bri, at anyone who would listen.

"I'm going to kill that crazy old bitch! Morna! Where the hell are you? On the other hand, you better run, because when I find you, I'm going to kick your ass! You said Bri was supposed to be here! Did you put the *Kool-Aid* in that chicken pot pie?"

My back was toward him, but I spun quickly when I heard his voice. Cheese and crackers, he was freaking beautiful.

"What is 'cooo-laid,' lass?"

I momentarily forgot to kick my feet and dipped beneath the surface shortly before popping back up to spit up more water. He was at my side in an instant, his firm hand yanking me upward.

"I'm fine. Thank you."

He reached up and dabbed at the wound on my head. "No, ye are no fine. Ye are bleeding, lass. Do ye need me to help ye to shore?"

I pulled away from him and started to swim. Gorgeous or not, bleeding or not, I didn't know this man, and I had a sneaking suspicion he was part of the *Kool-Aid* club, whoever he was. "No. I can make it just fine."

"As ye wish, but ye will let me see to it once we get on shore. Ye have no choice in the matter."

No choice, my ass. My head would stop bleeding, but my sanity grew more fragile with every second I spent in Scotland. I would find Bri and bounce.

He was a practiced swimmer and reached the shore minutes before me, but he obviously saw how much I didn't want his help. He remained waiting on the shore for me to arrive.

He stood there dripping wet, bare-chested, chiseled beyond belief, and wearing, I kid you not, a kilt. My stomach immediately felt swimmy, even though by this point I was pulling myself out of the water.

I saw his face in the middle of the pond and, while it was equally stunning, to see the package all together, half-naked and dripping, was enough to warm my freezing, wet skin through. His dark eyes slanted out at the ends just slightly, making him look serious and smoldering. His hair was dark brown blended with different shades of copper, making his wavy hair look shiny and alive. He had lots of it and, although cut short, the glorious mass hung loosely around his ears. Wet, wavy curls hung down into his face and eyes.

I shook my head. No matter how ridiculously handsome he was, he was obviously part of the lunatic gang. I twisted and reached behind me to wring out my hair. The long ringlets absorbed water like a towel and, as I squeezed, it poured from the red locks like a running faucet.

"That's some head of hair ye've got there, lass. 'Tis stunning."

"Umm...thanks. Now seriously, I did what the crazy bat asked. I got dressed in this ridiculous outfit, traveled out here, threw the damn rock, and somehow got in the water. Surely that's enough for you bastards to allow Bri to talk to me. If she seriously wants to stay here, fine, but I need to see her and speak to her."

He regarded me skeptically and grabbed my arm as he dragged me over to a small rock bench just a few feet in front of us. "Bastard, lass? I am no one of those. Ye must be thinking of me brothers, and ye must have hit yer head harder than ye thought for no only are ye bleeding, ye are speaking utter nonsense."

I briefly forgot about my head, but as I felt the blood trickle down my face, I reached up to touch the gash above my forehead and winced at the sting. "Ouch. Yep, that hurts like a bitch now."

"Now? Did it no hurt ye before, lass?"

He reached forward with his hand, gently wiping away the stickiness from my face. He had no cloth, save his kilt, but he seemed more worried about cleansing the blood from my face than the ick factor of getting it on his hands. "No, it didn't hurt before and it only hurts a little now. It's already about stopped bleeding I think. It's not a deep cut."

He crouched down so that he was eye level with me and continued to gently wipe away my face. By the time he reached the slash, it had stopped bleeding entirely.

"Ye're right, lass, and I'm glad for it. Sit here a moment, I'm just going to wash this off."

He jogged over to the water's edge, and rinsed his hands. Before returning to me, he met two horses who were headed in his direction. Gathering their reins, he walked them to my side and patted both gently. "They were worried for ye too, lass. They ran to your aide as soon as they heard yer screams. Now, what was it that ye were saying in the water? Did I hear ye mention, Bri? Do ye know her, lass?"

The relief at hearing Bri's name was instant. I couldn't have been more pleased. If he knew her, she had to be close. "Yes, I do, and I need to speak to her right away. Where is she?"

"No here, lass. She resides at Conall Castle and is married to me cousin, Eoin."

So much for relief. "You've got to be kidding me. That's what Morna said too, but she said that I would find her by throwing the damn rock into the pond here. Not that I believed her but I at least thought she was around here somewhere."

He crouched down once more, worry evident on his face. "Morna Conall? She's been dead many years."

I stood, angry as ever. He did the same and, although he towered over me, I rammed my fingers deep into his chest. "Look buster, I'm sick of this crap. Morna is alive and well, unfortunately. Not that she's going to stay that way for long. She's the one that brought me here, and she told me that I would find Bri. If Bri's not here, I'll tell you what's going to happen. You are going to walk around to wherever you keep cars around here, get one, and you will be taking me to wherever Bri is, right this instant."

He didn't budge as I pushed on him. Staring down at me, amusement danced in his eyes, "I doona know what a 'car' is."

I rolled my eyes and walked over to the horses. "Fine! Then get me on one of these bloody horses, and we'll ride there."

"Did ye say 'bloody' lass? Are ye from England? Ye

doona sound English?"

"No, I'm not from England! I'm from the States. I don't know why I said bloody. I've never said it before in my life. I'm tired, my entire body hurts, and I'm ready to get out of this episode of *The Twilight Zone*." My voice cracked, and I swallowed hard to keep from crying. I hated that every time I got this angry, I felt the need to cry. It immediately made me seem less forceful.

He walked up to me and hesitantly tried to wrap his arms around me in comfort, but I jerked away.

He exhaled loudly in surrender and when he spoke, his voice was sympathetic. "I'm verra sorry I've upset ye, lass. It wasna me intention. What's yer name?"

I sucked up my sniffles and tried to steady my voice. "Mitsy, and yours?"

"Baodan. Now, I believe that ye know Bri. By the way ye are going on about her, I have no doubt. I will take ye to see her but I'm afraid I canna do it right away."

A new voice answered him, and I turned to see another man approach. He was striking in the most unusual of ways. His hair matched my own in color and he was tall but didn't move as smoothly as Baodan, each step forward reserved and slightly hunched. His lips were large and one corner of them pulled, his voice exceedingly deep.

"No, brother, ye doona need to take her anywhere. Ye can leave her in me charge, and I will see her to Conall Castle meself."

Chapter 8

"What?" My voice broke, and blood ran to my face so quickly I thought my head might burst from the pressure of it. Enough was enough. "I'm not staying in anybody's 'charge.' I haven't joined your crazy role-playing, cult circus, so don't try to pull that load of bologna on me!"

I continued to scream, but neither man listened to me as they stared down one another. Finally, Baodan reached out and grabbed me firmly on the shoulder, pushing me soundly down into a sitting position on the bench. "Sit and hush. Doona say another word. Eoghanan needs to explain himself, and I canna hear him with yer screeching. Just calm down, lass."

I tried to stand but his hand still pressed on my shoulder. He was strong as a bull and I would go nowhere unless he allowed me to, but surely he couldn't keep me from talking. "Calm down? Are you crazy? You're both acting like I'm some sort of object!"

"Did I no just tell ye to hush? Would ye like me to gag ye, or will ye cease speaking on yer own?"

I crossed my arms and stayed silent, he was obviously serious and I had no desire to be muffled.

He faced the other man and, by the way he was staring at him, I got the impression he was nearly as angry as I.

"Just what do ye think ye are doing, Eoghanan? I wouldna leave ye to watch over a toad. I trusted ye once and it ended with me wife dead. I doona trust ye with women that belong to me."

"What?" I didn't care if he gagged me, he was out of his

mind. "You are a sick bastard. I've known you all of ten minutes. I do not belong to you."

Both men ignored me, and I drew my gaze to the pained expression on Eoghanan's face as he fidgeted uncomfortably.

"I am tired of this between us, brother. How can ye carry such hatred with ye for so long? 'Tis time for ye to put this behind us. Ye canna delay Mother's journey, and ye canna take this lass along with ye. If ye wish to be the one to take her to Conall Castle, then ye should be the one to do so. In the meantime, someone must look after her."

Baodan released his grip on my shoulder and stepped in front of me protectively. "And ye think that should be ye? Like hell."

I scooted over on the bench to watch the men intently, now intrigued. Fantastic actors, both of them. These guys took role-playing to a whole different level.

Eoghanan stepped forward, his voice low and just as angry as Baodan's. "Surely, ye doona mean to leave Niall to watch over her? He'll have her undressed and in his bed before sundown."

Baodan shook his head, glancing down at me. I assumed he meant to reassure me that he wouldn't let that happen. "I doona like it but ye are right. I canna leave her with Niall."

"Then give me a chance, brother. 'Tis no the same as it was with her and ye know it."

I very much wondered who "her" was, but neither man gave me a chance to ask.

Baodan all but growled at who apparently was his brother, although I seriously doubted they were related by blood. They didn't resemble each other in the slightest. "If anything happens to the lass, ye will no enjoy what happens to ye."

"Excuse me?" I hardly recognized my own voice, so screechy with rage. I stood and stepped out of his reach before he could grab my shoulder again and went to stand apart from them so that we made an odd sort of triangle. "Let me explain something. Nothing is going to happen because I am not staying here. I'm going to see Bri, and I don't need anything from you." I squirmed, suddenly needing to use the restroom. Damn bladder. Why did I always need to pee at the most inconvenient moments? "Except perhaps have you direct me to a toilet."

"A 'toilet'?" Both men said the word in unison.

I threw my hands up in exasperation. "Stop! Seriously, just cut it out. Press pause for just a moment. Once I'm where I need to be, you are free to resume this delusional little game of yours."

Eoghanan spoke only to Baodan. "Is the lass daft? What is she talking about?"

Baodan shook his head. "I doona think she's daft. She hit her head though, perhaps she just needs some rest."

"Aye, I believe she does. She looks a bit wild, does she no?"

Eoghanan glanced in my direction but tore his gaze away after he saw the glare I was giving him.

"Hello? Did either one of you hear what I just said? Of course I'm not daft, you bunch of morons! Quit ignoring me."

Again, neither heard nor listened to me. As I stared, their conversation quickly escalated into a full-out argument, and I stood back looking around at the castle grounds. I don't know why I didn't realize it after I got out of the water or even after I asked him to go and get a car, but as I noticed the utter lack of modern transportation, a sudden chill rushed down my spine.

When Morna pulled up in front of the pond, there had indeed been other vehicles at the castle, not around the pond where she parked, but up closer to the castle. A tourist attraction, just like Conall Castle and many of the castles in the surrounding area.

I wasn't sure how much time passed in between tossing the rock and waking in the water but it only felt like seconds, and it was still broad daylight. It couldn't possibly have been more than a few hours. Could the castle have closed for visitors in that time? If so, was it likely that every employee and security guard left as well?

Every second things just grew weirder, and I couldn't stand to be here a moment longer. I glanced over at the horses. They seemed gentle enough, and I'd been on horses a few times. Maybe if I silenced myself, I could get away atop one of them. Unlikely, but I couldn't just stand here staring at crazy one and crazy two.

Slowly, I backed away. Watching them argue, I crossed over to the horse farthest from them. I imagined I could see the chestnut colored mares' sympathy for me in her eyes. She would cooperate, if only the men would keep arguing long enough for me to get away.

It didn't work. Just as I jumped to wrap my arms around her so I could pull myself up, I heard Baodan turn as he addressed his brother. He'd known I meant to leave the second I started to back away.

"I'm going to see her to a room. Ye may make sure she's cared for, but doona let her outside of the room. I fear she'll try to leave if ye do so."

Before I could pull myself up on the horse, Baodan

grabbed me off the beast, flipping me over his shoulder so that my head bounced up and down against his back as he carried me off toward the castle.

Chapter 9

I stopped screaming once he stepped inside the main building. It did me no good anyway. He had a firm grip and, no matter how much I banged on him or hollered at the top of my lungs, he didn't release me. Besides, the interior of the castle was so beautiful and quiet, it seemed quite wrong to disturb the atmosphere by screaming.

My silence seemed to bother him, and he reached up with his left hand that he wrapped around my legs and gave me a quick smack on the rear. "Did ye lose consciousness, lass? I dinna know ye could be so quiet."

The smack elicited a yelp, and he laughed at the sound.

"Where are you taking me?" The words sounded broken, each step he took up the stairs knocking the air out of me.

"Did ye no just hear what I told Eoghanan? I'm taking ye to a bedchamber, where I will ravish ye before leaving on me journey."

"What?" Screaming once more, I lifted my left leg and swung it down into his lower stomach just as hard as I could. "You will do no such thing. Sit me down. Now!"

He grunted at the impact but laughed loudly, pinning my legs against him giving me no chance of kicking him again. "Shhh, lass, I jest. I promise I shan't touch ye. We are only going to have a little talk, ye and I."

"I don't want to talk. All I want is to find Bri, shake the crazy out of her, and then get on a plane back to the States."

He stopped in front of a large door and released the grip on my legs with one of his hands so that he could open it.

Once inside, he closed the door and set me down on my feet. Dizzy from being upside down, my head also pounded from the injury. He reached out to steady me as I got my bearings. "I doona know what a 'plane' is, lass. Just like I dinna know what a 'car' was when ye mentioned it earlier."

I pulled away from him once my blood seemed to be running in the right direction. "Right, I forgot. We're in the past. Do they have like cameras watching you guys all the time and if you break character they put you in a dungeon or something?"

Baodan squinted his brows at me and went to sit in a large chair across the room. "Ye are verra strange, lass. Half of what ye say seems like another language entirely. Why doona ye take a seat?"

I didn't know if it was from hanging upside down, my confusion and rage, or just because it was genuinely warm in the room, but I grew very warm. With a head wound, I thought I better be careful. "I'm really hot. Can you maybe turn up the air in here a bit?"

Again, the same confused expression. I wanted to knock it off of his pretty face.

"I could open a window if ye like?"

I pinched my dress in between my boobs and lifted it up and down quickly to fan myself. Baodan regarded me as if I was doing a strip tease in front of him. "Yes, please do, but can you adjust the thermostat? Hasn't this place been modernized? If you have visitors everyday, surely it has air conditioning."

As he opened the window, I moved around the room looking for air vents. With the exception of the window, no source of circulation could be found anywhere in the room. I hadn't noticed right away, but light from outside illuminated the room, not electricity. Sunlight and candles were the only source of light.

"Where did ye say ye came from? What is a 'thermostat'?"

The only explanation I could think of was that they'd not modernized anything to preserve the historical value of the place. Regardless, it seemed odd that there wouldn't be the slightest hint of anything modern in the room.

"I'm from the United States, and I live in Texas. I'm from the same place as Bri." I moved to sit in the chair across from him. My head was starting to ache again from the cut.

Baodan leaned forward so that his elbows rested on his knees, and he clasped his hands out in front of himself, regarding me sternly. "Well, ye see lass, now ye have given me cause to worry over ye, for ye are either one of two things. Ye are either daft, as Eoghanan suggests, or ye are a liar."

"Excuse me?" I leaned my elbow against the arm of the chair and allowed the side of my face to rest inside my palm.

"Aye, lass, now which is it? Bri doesna come from this place that ye speak of. She is the daughter of Laird MacChristy, a twin to be exact, although few people knew he had two daughters until recently. While I'll admit that ye speak much like her, she spent her childhood living in many different places, traveling with a relative of her father. I doona know her well, but I have met her, and I know this to be true."

I sat up and leaned forward so that we stared squarely at one another. "You don't know squat, because all of that's not even remotely true. I can't imagine why she would have made that up, maybe you have to tell a cool story to get into this club, but it's seriously time to give me a break. Haven't I been through enough today? I got dressed up in this ridiculous garment, I rode all the way out here only to be knocked unconscious and somehow dropped into the middle of the pond out there, I cut open my head, and now I'm held against my will. Please. I am begging you, just cut the crap and tell me what's really going on here." I tried to look as desperate as possible, not that I found it hard to do. I started to feel panicked about the inconsistencies of everything that went on around me. None of it made any sense.

He reached forward and grabbed both my hands, his touch gentle. I didn't have enough fight left to pull away. It reassured me to know that despite how crazy he seemed, he genuinely felt sympathetic to my plight.

"Lass, I doona know what ye wish for me to tell ye. Why doona ye ask me a direct question, and I will do me best to answer it. But doona use the strange words ye've been using or I willna be able to help ye a bit."

"Fine." I moved around in the chair, unable to get comfortable. With my dress still very wet, it grew heavy. "For starters, is there any woman around from whom I could borrow some clothes? Jeans would be nice, but if you all insist that I wear another costume dress like this, I guess it will suffice."

He looked nearly as tired as I felt. "Ye did it again. 'Jeans?' I doona know what those are. I will send for someone to bring ye a new dress just as soon as I leave ye."

"Leave? You said you would take me to Bri."

"That I did, but ye are forgetting that I told ye I canna do it right away. I have promised me mother that I would see her to my aunt's and that I shall. It should take me no more than three or four days. Upon me return, I will take ye to Bri at once."

I crossed my legs and arms while shaking my head. "Are you suggesting that I stay here for four days while you're gone? You're crazy. That is so not going to happen. You said she's at Conall Castle, right?"

He glanced down at my chest disapprovingly, and I rolled my eyes. Crossing my arms pushed up my breasts and emphasized the cleavage in the dress.

"While I doona believe ye are from where ye say ye are, I do believe that ye doona come from here. I havena seen a lass sit like that in me entire life."

Just to aggravate him, I squeezed my arms together, just briefly, to make them stand out even more. "Good grief. They're just boobs, and what do you expect when the dresses are cut to hold them in like they're being served on a platter?"

He laughed loudly, a deep, belly laugh so contagious I couldn't help but smile in return.

"I dinna say that I doona enjoy the sight of them, but ye would be asking for trouble in the wrong company. 'Tis lucky that I found ye in the pond and no Niall and, aye, Bri is at Conall Castle."

"Great! Then I don't need anyone to accompany me. It will take me all day, but I'm pretty sure I can find my way there on my own."

"I'm afraid 'tis no possible, lass."

A knock on the door interrupted us, and the oldest looking woman I'd ever seen stuck her head inside the door.

"Yer, mother is awake and ready to leave as soon as possible." The woman glanced over in my direction and took in the puddle forming at both our feet. "I'll bring the lass a new dress at once. Will she be staying here?"

I stood and moved toward her. "No, I'm leaving as soon

67

as I get a change of clothes."

She paid me no mind, looking through me as if I'd said nothing. "Baodan?"

"Aye, she will stay in this room until I return. I have left her in Eoghanan's care, mistake it may be, but please have men stay close to the door at all times, and make sure that she is well cared for."

The woman nodded and left, closing the door behind her. I made to follow her but Baodan quickly moved to block me, looming in the doorway. "I'm sorry, lass, but ye willna be leaving without me. 'Tis too far to Conall Castle for ye to travel alone, and I doona trust me brothers to see ye all the way there."

"Why?" He spoke of his brothers as if they were criminals. I didn't have much experience with siblings or normal families myself, but his mistrust of them seemed odd.

"Eoghanan is negligent, and Niall would seek to woo and take ye for the sport of it. No, that ye will have a choice in it, but promise me that ye willna leave this room until I return."

"You're joking? I will do no such thing." I tried to step around him, but he grabbed both of my arms, holding me still out in front of him.

"Aye lass, ye will."

"Look, I appreciate your concern, but you don't need to worry about your brothers. I don't need someone to look out for me so even if Eoghanan is 'negligent' it won't be a problem, and I am not all that woo-able so neither with Niall. While none of you seem to be, I am living in the twenty-first century and, just FYI, it's completely illegal to keep me here against my will."

Genuine worry spread across his face, and he released his

grip on my arms. He seemed very sad for me, and it made something deep within me hurt. I didn't want his pity, especially without reason for it.

"Ach, so Eoghanan was right then? Ye are daft. If that be the case, then I am sure ye are truly verra scared. I am verra sorry for that, lass, but 'tis all the more reason for me to keep ye here. Ye are right when ye say that ye are no mine in the way that ye meant, but ye are mine to care for ye until I deliver ye safely into someone else's hands."

He ran his hand down my arm like you would someone ill. It only served to infuriate me more. "What? You seriously think I'm crazy, don't you? Well, I've got news for you, buddy. I am not the crazy one. Quit eating the food here, seriously, they are screwing with your head and you my friend, are the one who has lost it."

He smiled at me pathetically and reached for the door. "Ye shall be well taken care of while I am away. When I return, we will travel to Bri's. Perhaps she will know where and to whom ye belong."

With that, he left the room, locking it securely behind him. I couldn't begin to process all that just happened. Part of me wanted to laugh hysterically at his assumption but, at this point, I started to feel sort of crazed myself. Maybe the blow on the head confused me somewhat.

Only a few minutes later, the woman who entered earlier opened the door to extend a fresh dress in my direction. She said nothing and didn't enter the room. As soon as I'd grabbed it from her, she closed the door and locked it.

I stripped quickly, eager to get dry and ready to rip open the pouch with the medicine. Morna had been right about one thing. I needed something to ease my aching head. The fact that she'd known I would require it disturbed and puzzled me to no end.

Turning the dress inside out, I pulled at the loose stitching around the pouch. It came open easily. Inside was a small plastic case filled with much-needed ibuprofen. Something else lay in the pouch, and I had to reach inside to grab it. As soon as my fingers touched the smooth, cold surface, bile built up in the back of my throat.

I pulled the object out and threw it onto the bed, truly frightened for the first time since the beginning of all this craziness. In the center of the bed now sat the shiny, black rock. The rock I sent skipping all the way to the bottom of the pond.

Chapter 10

They reached the castle grounds three days after leaving home. Baodan couldn't help but notice that his mother seemed far less tired than he. While he took care with her, traveling much more slowly than he wished, she should not have been so full of life this far into their journey.

He couldn't make sense of it, but Eoghanan was right. All it took was half a day's ride and a shabby meal of pheasant to bring his mother back to her old self. She was still weak to be sure but, for the first time in months, light filled her eyes and she started talking as if she'd been starved of it for far too long.

They'd decided to bypass Cameron Castle itself, riding instead straight for his Aunt Nairne's cottage so that he could settle his mother and leave at once for home. His mother could greet his cousins later in the evening, but the journey took longer than he'd planned. He was anxious to check on Mitsy.

What a strange lass. Completely mad, but he couldn't help but like her. Perhaps all of her confusion could be put to her injured head, and he would return to find her at rights with herself.

He surely hoped so, for it seemed wrong of him to think of someone who was out of her mind in the way he thought about her. He spent every moment since leaving his home thinking of that mess of red curls and her whip-like mouth. He dreamed of tugging hard on those locks while claiming every inch of her lips with his own.

"I wish I hadna been sleeping so that I could have witnessed the arrival of the fiery lass who has so captured yer attention." His mother laughed as she looked behind her horse at him. Baodan believed she could read minds. "I am worried for her is all."

"I doona believe ye, although ye worry too much over everyone. The one ye should be worrying about is yerself."

Baodan nudged his horse forward so that he rode next to his mother rather than behind her. "Why do ye say that?"

"Because ye are in danger of growing hard hearted, me son. Ye have seen more loss and anguish than most, but life is no worth living if ye close yerself off from it."

He didn't answer her. Even if he wished to change, he didn't know how.

"That's all I'll say to ye about it. Now, tell me more about this girl. Ye said that she spoke of being from the twenty-first century?"

Baodan shook his head and smiled thinking back on it. The lass had a grand imagination, mad or no. "Aye, but she hit her head on a rock moments before. Perhaps it did more damage than she believed or than I realized at the time?"

His mother looked over at him and grinned nervously. "I swear to ye that me head is fine. I dinna bump it and I doona wish for ye to start to think that I am mad as well, but why are ye so inclined no to believe her?"

Surely she played some sort of trick on him. "Heh? I'm sorry, but what do ye mean by that? O'course I wasna inclined to believe her."

"Dinna ye say that she said many words for things that ye have never heard of?"

"Aye." He pulled back on the reins, slowing his horse. They grew close to his aunt's cottage, and he wanted to hear what his mother had to say before they arrived.

"And dinna ye say that she mentioned a woman named Morna? Yer uncle Alasdair's sister's name was Morna, and she was a powerful witch."

Baodan heard stories of her as a child, but most of his life he'd dismissed them as simple tales. He'd never heard his mother speak as if she believed the rumor to be true. "She isna a real witch, surely?"

"Aye son, a real witch. I dinna believe the stories either, no until our last visit to Conall Castle. Mary, ye remember her, doona ye? She told me the truth of it all. Bri is no more Laird MacChristy's daughter than old Heather here." She reached down to pat her horse. "She fell prey to a spell put in place by Morna many years ago, and as a result, she fell through time. 'Tis a verra long story and, to be honest, I doona remember all of it, but I spent enough time around yer cousin's strange wife to believe her story. She is kind and has made a place for herself amongst the family, but 'tis verra clear that neither her nor the lass' mother grew up in the same world as ye and I."

Impossible. No matter how odd the lass seemed, he'd never witnessed such magic himself. "Surely, ye canna mean it? How can something so impossible be so?"

"How can the love of two people create another? I doona see how that is any less impossible than this. I have seen magic in me life, son. It does exist, and there is a piece of it held captive in yer home. We are nearly there. I think it best if ye unload me horse and leave for home at once, for ye owe the lass a grand apology."

* * *

McMillan Castle

The smug, beautiful bastard lied. It was the fourth night since he locked me inside this room, and he'd still not returned. Not only that, but his idea of me being "well taken care of" differed from my own. Breakfast consisted of some sort of roasted bird. Unless, it poured out of a green box and tasted like sugary apples topped with milk, it didn't constitute breakfast.

Lunch and dinner could hardly be called that. Even if they'd been decent meals, they were still two meals less than what I usually ate a day. I liked to eat and made sure that I could keep doing so by running my fair share of miles everyday.

The exception being the last four days I'd spent locked up inside this hole. Perhaps hole was a bit extreme. I'd slept in few rooms as pretty and the bed, despite being springless and slightly lumpy, I found quite comfortable. All that aside, any room where I had to go to the bathroom inside a wooden bucket and use scraps of cloth as toilet paper, I could label as a hole.

I spent the first day in denial, clinging on to my hope that all of this was just some sort of nerdy role-playing game taken to the extreme, but by day two, I could no longer deny the unexplainable presence of the rock inside my dress and abandoned that notion. Only two other possibilities remained.

One: the impact of the water and the bump on my head had caused brain damage, and I truly was crazy. Two: Bri, Morna, and Jerry all told the truth.

The first possibility surprisingly seemed less plausible to

me than the second. After the first day, my headache was gone and I seemed to be having no sort of other cognitive difficulties. No slurred speech, no dizziness or confusion. Nothing. Only a small scab remained to remind me of the injury.

The second possibility, while admittedly insane, was now what I accepted as reality.

Bri was smart, and not the sort of person to easily fall under the influence of others. I'd used the assumption that Bri was crazy to rationalize the truth of something I simply couldn't wrap my head around.

Truthfully, I was no stranger to magic, the paranormal, or whatever you wanted to call it. In the end, my absolute certainty that I had the rock in my possession and two things that happened to me in my past finally made me accept the fact that I truly had landed in the seventeenth century.

The first happened when I was eighteen. On the day of my high school graduation, I walked up the steps to the front door of the only real home I'd ever known to collect my foster mother, Lilly, for the ceremony. With my hand on the knob, I twisted it, but for some reason the door simply wouldn't open. I tried over and over, but it wouldn't budge. Suddenly, I heard a voice, clear as day as if someone were right beside me. I glanced over my shoulder but found no one. Again I heard the same words. *"Don't go into the house alone. Call Jep and wait for him to get here."*

I started to cry. Since the door wouldn't budge, I did as the voice insisted. Once Jep arrived, the door opened with ease. Inside, we found the remnants of a break-in, with things smashed and broken everywhere, anything worth value stolen.

We called the police immediately, and Lilly arrived at the

house with them. Thankfully, she'd been out getting her hair done during the robbery. From a surveillance camera of a neighbor's house, the men had been armed and the time stamp showed they were still inside when I arrived at the front door. The thieves fled out the back.

The other incident occurred in college. During Winter Break, Lilly took me to Wales. Her parents moved from Wales to the States when she was a little girl, and she'd always wanted to make a trip back there to revisit her childhood. It was the most terrifying experience of my entire life.

We spent the day driving through Snowdonia National Park and decided to stop for the night at a small family run inn in a nearly deserted town. With the hotel virtually empty, we were the only one in a room on our side of the old house.

The evening passed normally and both of us slept like exhausted and weary travelers. But in the morning, things changed. We packed our bags, rolled them to the door, and opened it to see a figure staring at us not ten feet down the hallway.

The ghost stared at us as we stood frozen in the doorway, seemingly deciding if she approved of our presence. Neither of us breathed. After a few very long seconds, the woman turned and walked down the hallway, evaporating in the distance. If Lilly hadn't seen it also, I would have been certain I imagined it.

Both instances couldn't be explained, yet I knew with absolute certainty that both happened. Confident in the reality of those instances, I didn't see how I could continue to deny the possibility that something truly unexplainable happened here as well.

If I believed without doubt in guardian angels and ghosts,

why couldn't I believe in time travel?

Chapter 11

I woke on the fifth morning with a fully renewed attitude about my current situation. Sure, it terrified me to realize that I'd somehow ended up in a time nearly four hundred years before I was born, but I also had hope that when I was ready to return, I would be able to. After all, I had the rock, didn't I?

According to Morna, the entire purpose of the rock depended on it. So far she'd told the truth about almost everything. Skipping the rock indeed sent me back in time and the rock magically returned to me after I tossed it, just as she'd promised it would. Bri, however, Morna lied about. While Baodan confirmed that she lived in this time as well, the innkeeper made it seem like I would find her here at McMillan Castle, and Bri wasn't. She probably didn't even know that I was here in this time with her.

I twirled the rock in between my fingers. It scared the bejeezus out of me to find it inside the pouch, but now I prized my possession of it as my lifeline back to home. As long as I had that with me, I saw no reason not to enjoy my time spent with Bri in a place and time most people would only ever dream of visiting. I might as well enjoy this place as well, until Baodan took me to Conall Castle.

I slipped out of the gown I'd been given to sleep in and reluctantly crawled back into the now-dry gown that I traveled here in. I found it uncomfortable, which made me self-conscious. I was a jeans and a t-shirt, sweats and hoodie kind of girl. Dresses were no less than a tolerable form of torture.

I spent half of an entire day trying to figure out how to do up the laces myself. While I figured out how to keep the dress up, it was sloppy work. As long as I wouldn't reveal myself to the man sitting outside my door, I felt satisfied.

Walking across the room, I knocked at the door and tried to rouse Eoghanan. I knew he sat just outside the door. He spent every moment leaning against the doorway since Baodan left. Until now, I'd only managed to get a few words out of him. I intended to change that today.

"E-o, look. In case you haven't noticed, your name isn't the easiest to pronounce so I'm just going to call you, E-o. Is that cool?" As expected, he didn't answer, and I slumped down in the doorway and sat with my shoulder leaning against the hinge. "Come on. I know you're out there. I see you every time a meal's brought, or a bath, or they come to empty my chamber pot. You haven't left, not even at night. I can hear your snoring through the door. Open up. I won't try to leave, I swear. I just want to talk."

He groaned, annoyed, but still said nothing.

"You have no idea what a talker I can be, and I have nothing to do in here. So you can either open up this door and talk to me for a little bit or you can sit there with the door closed and listen to me talk at you all day long."

"Ye doona need the door open to speak to me, lass. If ye insist on doing so, talk as ye are now."

I shook my head, stopping when I realized that, of course, he couldn't see me do it. "Nope. I'm afraid that's not going to work for me. I like to speak to people face to face, not through big wooden doors."

He laughed, but I could tell I made him uncomfortable. I really didn't care.

"I doona think Baodan would want me talking to ye,

lass."

"I don't give a damn what Baodan wants. I'm being held in here like a prisoner when I've done nothing wrong. The least you could do is open the door and talk to me."

I heard him stand and I smiled. I could out-pester anybody. Although I knew I shouldn't pride myself on it, I usually got what I wanted.

He shouted and I jumped, but it wasn't at me. He told the guards at either end of the hallway to stand down. "If she tries to run, stop her lads. I only mean to talk to her." After a moment of no movement, I heard him slip the key inside and open the door.

Seeing me sitting on the floor, he did the same, mirroring my position so that we faced each other, each of us leaning against the inside of the door frame.

"Thank you." I smiled and leaned across him to peek down the hallway, but he quickly grabbed my arms and pushed me back inside.

"Did ye no just tell me that ye wouldna try to leave? I'll no hesitate to shut the door again and leave ye to talk with only yerself."

"I wasn't trying to leave, I just wanted to see what it looked like. All I saw was the upside-down view. It's beautiful."

He nodded and looked up and around him as if he hadn't taken the time to appreciate its beauty in some time. "Aye, lass, it is. Now what do ye wish to speak about?"

Where to begin? Anxious to ask many things, I decided to start with what pressed at the forefront of my mind. "Why have you been sitting outside my door? Caring for me and being a creepy stalker are two very different things."

"I'm sitting out here for yer protection."

"Why?"

"Because ye doona want the men of this castle to enter yer room."

I crossed my arms but quickly uncrossed them, remembering Baodan's reaction. The fact that I allowed Baodan to see, but wouldn't let Eoghanan game me a moment of pause.

"What does that mean? Are you saying that I need to be protected from you?"

He shook his head and looked down at his hands awkwardly. "No, lass. I swear to ye I willna hurt ye."

"Then who? The other brother? Niall, is that his name?"

"Ye are no afraid to say whatever ye think. 'Tis unusual in a lass."

"Sorry." I wasn't sorry at all. I had no filter, and I didn't imagine that would change anytime soon.

"Doona be sorry, I doona suppose anyone ever has to fear that ye are pretending to be someone ye are no and that's more than most people can say."

"Yes, it's a problem. What's Baodan's problem with you?"

He hesitated as if deciding to share that information, then relented. "He believes that I am responsible for a great hurt, and foolishly he doesna trust me."

E-o wouldn't hurt me. I'd spent all of five minutes with him, and I would stake my life on that fact. A pain in his green eyes made my chest hurt, but a deeply rooted kindness lived within him. A kindness I expected he'd been unable to express for some time. "He's wrong about you."

He looked up from his hands at me and smiled, obviously

surprised. "Why would ye say that, lass? Ye doona know me at all."

I shrugged my shoulders and grinned at him. "I have a knack for that sort of thing. I'm good at reading people." I thought of Brian and grimaced. "Well, most people anyway."

He laughed and I saw his smile for the first time. Large and crooked, his lower lip stuck out in the most adorable way. What could he possibly have done to make Baodan despise him so much?

"Ah, well we all have pasts, doona we? By the look on yer face, I can see ye are thinking about someone in yer's."

"Yes, but it's nothing worth thinking about. Can I ask you a question?"

"Aye, for ye will anyway."

"You're not really his brother are you?"

He turned quite pale but recovered quickly. It couldn't have been that big of a secret. I'd not met Niall yet, but Baodan had dark hair and eyes. E-o looked more like he could've been my brother, with the same red hair and skin tone as myself.

"I am in every way that matters, lass, but ye are right. I am no his brother by blood."

He didn't seem to want to elaborate so I didn't press him. "Can I ask you just one more? Last one, I swear."

"Aye."

"Is Baodan wrong about Niall as well?"

Anger flashed across his face, and I knew his answer before he spoke. "No, if anything, Baodan doesna realize how dangerous Niall can be."

"And that's why you sit outside here?"

He nodded somberly. "Aye, but lass," he paused and

reached out to grab my hand. "I'm afraid I willna be here tonight. There is something I must attend to before Baodan's return. I shall lock yer bedchamber door, and Rhona will have the only other key. I am sure that I have been over-cautious. Doona worry. The guards will be outside yer doorway as well."

Suddenly chilled, I nodded and pulled my hands away from him to run my hands up and down my sleeves as I watched him stand to leave. "What is it that you have to do?"

He shut the door, and I could hear his footsteps fading away along with the sound of his voice. "I'm afraid that I canna tell ye that. And lass...please doona call me E-o, I'll teach ye how to properly say me name next time I see ye."

I laughed as his footsteps retreated, any worry that I'd felt due to his concern for my safety gone as quickly as it came.

* * *

Eoghanan reached the alchemist's cottage by sunset. As he slipped off his horse, he led the beast to the back, securing it safely out of sight so that none would see him.

He could see the old man working inside. He was alone, just as he'd hoped. The man appeared small and frail. It wouldn't be difficult to overpower him, but Eoghanan hoped he wouldn't put up a fight. He wished to hurt the alchemist as little as possible.

Peeking around the corner of the home to make sure that no one watched, he stepped inside without knocking. Approaching him from behind, he raised his fist and brought it down hard upon the back of the man's head.

One blow was all it took. Catching him as he went limp, Eoghanan gathered his target and strapped him to the back of his horse then rode in the direction of McMillan Castle's dungeons.

Chapter 12

My stomach growled loudly, reminding me that it was past time for another measly meal of some sort of meat I would unlikely want to eat. Usually food arrived right at sunset, but the sun set hours ago, and my stomach rumbled in response to it.

Just as I contemplated whether I should holler at one of the guards to see what the hang up was, I heard the key jiggle inside the lock. I moved to a small table against the farthest wall of the room and sat with my back to the door to await my food.

The door latched into place, and I froze in my seat. Rhona never stayed long enough to bother closing the door. I knew before I turned that it was not her in the room with me. I'd nearly forgotten Eoghanan's warning and the concern on his face at having to leave me alone but, as rocks settled in my stomach, I knew who I would find as I twisted in my chair.

"You must be Niall."

He nodded as he moved to set the food down in front of me and then went to lean against the wall beside the small table so that he looked right at me.

I expected him to be tall and menacing. Instead, he stood much shorter than both Baodan and Eoghanan and his face was unusually pretty for a male. He was good looking, no doubt, and he knew it too. He displayed it in the way he held himself. I suspected he denied himself little.

"Aye, lass, right ye are. 'Tis a pleasure to finally meet she who has all in the castle busy with gossip."

Unlike the ease I felt with both other brothers, I held my breath in Niall's presence. I wondered if I would have felt the same way if Eoghanan withheld his warning. Regardless, something inside told me to tread carefully. "Where's Rhona? She usually brings me my meals."

He waved his hand dismissively and stepped closer in my direction. "Eat, lass. Rhona dinna feel well, so she went abed and left yer meal in the hand of her kitchen maid. I told her I'd be happy to take it to ye as I was anxious to introduce meself. When I arrived, I found that both the guards were no feeling so well either. Seems something has spread throughout the castle."

"Ah." I ate slowly, hardly looking up from my plate in the hopes that he would take his leave. Inside, I knew better. If he had any intention of leaving, he wouldn't have closed the door behind him.

He waited until I finished. With every bite, I could see his eyes raking over me. All my hunger vanished, and each bite was a struggle. I no longer wished to eat.

"Thank you for the food." I stood from the table and moved to the door to open it for him. "I'm quite tired. If you don't mind, I think I'll retire now."

I only just cracked the door open before his long strides met me as he pushed it closed with his hand. "Just a moment. I willna trouble ye long." He reached to grab a small satchel hanging off of his kilt and dropped it onto the table where I'd just eaten. The bag jingled with coins, and I swallowed a hard lump in my throat.

"What's that for?"

"'Tis yer payment, o'course. There is talk around the castle that yer trade is in the company of men. I doona usually

86

have use for such women, but I heard ye were verra pretty. And ye are."

He stepped closer and grabbed me by the arm. He touched me gently, but a threat lay within it, a dare to pull away.

I stayed still but turned my head away as he leaned in to caress a handful of my hair. "Why would they say that? Obviously it isn't true. I'm a friend of the Conalls and am only staying here until Baodan returns. Then he is going to escort me to see them."

He stepped toward the bed and held onto me so that I moved with him. "I doona believe ye, lass. 'Tis true that castle servants often form untruths to entertain themselves, but I see no other reason for ye to be here."

"I just told you the other reason. I'm on my way to the Conalls."

"Enough!"

Deep and angry, his voice spread goose bumps over my entire body.

"If that were true, ye wouldna be traveling alone. Now, ye have received yer payment, and I will receive me purchase."

He moved the hand entangled in my hair to the base of my neck and twisted my head until I had no choice but to face him. I closed my eyes, trying to think of what I should do.

His mouth moved to my ear, and he whispered breathlessly into it. Warm breath touched my skin, but it sent ice crystals running down my spine.

"This can be enjoyable for us both, lass, if ye let it. I am no a selfish lover and while I know some men doona mind being met with a struggle, 'tis no something I prefer. But struggle or no, I shall have ye. Make up yer mind which it shall be now."

He waited for me to answer, breathing down my neck while pushing himself into my stomach. His words offered me solution. He enjoyed being a charmer. He took his pleasure by giving pleasure. He enjoyed the act of leaving women with hope when there was none.

I was strong, but he would be able to overpower me if I struggled. If I could pretend to want him until I made him vulnerable, perhaps I could injure him enough to escape.

Terrified, my hands trembled, but I knew if I cried I would lose my nerve. I needed to give an Oscar-worthy performance. Clenching my hands into fists to still them, I moved them up to his wrists, gently tugging at them so he would release my neck.

He did and looked at me curiously, anxious for me to give him an answer. I stepped away from him and smiled as seductively as I could. "Have you ever done this before? Paid for someone I mean?"

"No."

His answer pleased me. It meant he wouldn't be accustomed to a woman who knew anything about sex. He most likely spent his nights with virgins. His eyes danced with anticipation. I knew if I could just pull it off, I would be able to get away.

"Always more of a giver than a receiver, yes?"

"Aye."

He spoke breathlessly, and he looked as if he would start foaming at the mouth any minute. Disgusted with myself, I was about to throw up, but I would not allow him to have the upper hand in this situation. "Well, then I think it's time somebody focused on you. What do you say? Take off your kilt."

He stared at me, clearly shocked, and the lust in his eyes disappeared. I worried I'd taken it too far.

"What about yer dress, lass? This hardly seems fair."

"I'll take my clothes off in a little bit, after I've sated you." He seemed to like that answer and stripped quickly. Once naked, he charged me, crushing his mouth to mine as he moved me on top of the bed, pinning me with his body.

He was so ravenous with his mouth that I could hardly breathe. It took all my concentration not to gag. He thought himself better at this than he truly was. Every woman he'd ever been with must have been mighty inexperienced to find that sort of mouth exploration appealing.

He reached his hand underneath my dress, and I threw my hand down to stop him. "Not so fast. Your turn first."

He grinned and moved to kiss my ear, laughing at the delight of something unexpected. Thankfully, he couldn't see my face, for I shut my eyes as I reached down to grab him, dreading the sensation. I opened my eyes and rolled them as I latched on. I found very little to grab. No wonder he felt the need to overcompensate in the way he moved and talked. There was no way he didn't feel a little self-conscious about all that didn't hang between his legs.

He groaned, and his entire stomach clenched as I stroked him. I concentrated all my energy toward the door, trying to calculate just how quickly I could reach it. As he moaned louder, I knew I would have no chance if I allowed him to finish. I slowed my pace to torture him before following through with my plan.

He reacted as I expected, and he rocked against me when I slowed.

"Doona stop, lass."

"Okay." Reaching down with my other hand, I picked up my pace once again and counted to three under my breath. At three, I yanked on his testicles with one hand and his shaft with the other as hard as I could.

Nervous and frightened, I pulled harder than intended and found myself halfway surprised the whole appendage didn't just fall off in my hand.

I expected him to scream and then roll over on his side in the hopes that he would stay down long enough for me to escape, but my plan worked even better than I imagined. Scream he did, but only for a moment. Then he just turned white and his eyes rolled up into his head as he passed out cold on top of me.

Chapter 13

What on earth was the lass doing, and why didn't it surprise him that she'd chosen not to wait for him and managed to escape? Baodan just rounded the edge of the pond when he saw her running as fast as she could go into the woods, her red curls bouncing messily out behind her. He'd never seen a woman move so quickly in his entire life.

He called out to her as he approached but, instead of slowing, he watched her pick up her speed as she turned to him.

Worry gripped him, something happened to upset her greatly.

"Come on, Artair, we need to reach her." The horse sped up as he bid.

* * *

As soon as I rolled out from under the shockingly un-endowed creep, I grabbed my shoes and Morna's rock and took off from the castle at full speed. I knew he would send someone after me, but it wouldn't be Niall himself. I expected he would be out of commission for a while.

It felt good to run, and as the cool evening air hit my lungs, I delighted in the pleasant sting with each breath I took.

I neared the edge of the castle grounds when I saw the horse approaching, but it was too dark for me to tell the rider's identity. I assumed one of the guards found me. I pushed myself to run faster although I knew I wouldn't be able to outrun the horse.

Eventually, the horse followed close behind me, and I could clearly hear the voice of its rider. Baodan.

"Mitsy, just who do ye think ye are running from? There's no one coming after ye."

I slowed to a jog and then to a walk so that I moved right beside him and the horse. "You are. And there is no way in hell that I am going back inside that castle. If you try to make me, I'll do the same thing I just did to your scum bag of a brother. Then, I'll steal your horse so I don't have to walk all the way to Conall Castle."

"What?" Panic filled his voice.

I heard him jump off his horse as he rushed to stand in front of me. It forced me to stop and, as I did so, he reached out to grab both of my arms. "Let go," I demanded.

He did so immediately, but didn't allow me to move around him.

"Lass, ye must tell me what ye mean. Did he hurt ye? I swear I'll kill him if he did."

I wasn't going to stop until I was far away from McMillan Castle. I didn't want to talk about it anyway, not tonight. If he wanted to know, he would have to keep travelling right along with me. I'd tell him after I cooled down a little. "Are you going to take me to Conall Castle? And I mean like right now, because I'm not stopping until I'm far away from here."

"Aye, lass. If ye wish it, we shall ride through the night and rest in the morning but, for God's sake, tell me what happened to upset ye so."

He walked backward and was about to trip over a stump, so I stopped for a moment and reached out to grab his hand to steady him. He mistook my reach as a desire to draw him near, and he deftly laced his fingers with mine, stepping forward to pull me into an embrace. "What happened, lass?"

I knew if things had turned out differently with Niall, I would have flinched at Baodan's touch, but mercifully they hadn't and I welcomed Baodan's embrace. He carried no agenda behind it. He worried for me, and held me because it wasn't in his nature to do otherwise.

I sighed, laying my head against his chest. With the adrenaline rush of earlier subsiding, I suddenly grew tired. "If it's ok, I don't want to talk about it right now. If you'll take me to Conall Castle, I'll tell you in the morning."

"If ye insist, though I wish ye would tell me now. I willna press ye. Come." He grabbed my hand and led me to the horse. Lifting me up on the horse first, he then swung himself over so that he sat behind me.

He didn't hesitate to slip both of his arms around my waist. After gathering the reins, Baodan placed the side of his hands directly on my thighs, holding the leather straps perilously close to the center of my legs. I gasped at the sensation. It felt oddly intimate, but he didn't pull away nor did he act as if he were doing anything unusual.

He wiggled the reins to nudge the horse forward. Once we moved, he extended his hand to pat my knee quickly. "Ye are tense, lass. I willna let ye fall off." He squeezed his arms around me to emphasize his point. "Lean against me and go to sleep."

I did allow myself to relax and happily leaned against him but, while I was exhausted, I knew I wouldn't be able to sleep. Not right away. "I'm not sleepy."

"Aye, ye are. I'm sorry that I dinna return as quickly as I thought I would. Me mother was ill, and it slowed us down a bit."

I didn't say anything. He couldn't help his mother's ill health, but I couldn't bring myself to say it was alright. If he'd returned when he said, Eoghanan wouldn't have had to leave and Niall would never have approached me.

He reached up to touch my hairline, to examine my injury. "'Tis no so bad as it looked that first day. Does it hurt ye, lass?"

I shook my head lightly. "Not at all. Just a little scab now."

"Good. I'm pleased to hear it."

We rode in silence for a while. I spent the hours looking up at the stars, picking out constellations in awe. A million changes would occur in the time that spanned from the year I found myself in now to the time I was born in. Everything would change, everything except the stars.

"What are ye looking at, lass?"

He leaned forward and whispered the words in my ear. Unlike his brother's breath that chilled me to my bones, the sound of his deep whisper warmed me all the way to my core.

"The stars. They look exactly the same three hundred and sixty-seven years from now. Well, I'm sure an astrologist would tell you they've changed a little, but I sure can't tell a difference."

His breath caught as I spoke, and I cringed as I awaited more accusations of my insanity. I'd forgotten that he'd thought me 'daft.'

"Tell me more about your time. What are some of the things ye mentioned before? A plane and a car? What is a toilet?"

I twisted my head to look at him with pinched brows. "What? When you left you thought I was crazy. What happened?"

He laughed and I didn't miss how his eyes lingered on my lips before he glanced upward again. I turned my head back around to face the direction of our travel.

"Aye, lass, I truly did, but me mother told me the truth. I informed her how ye screamed after someone named Morna when I found ye in the pond, and she knows of the woman's power. Morna's been dead a long time, but she was a powerful witch. Mother told me of all that the witch did to bring yer friend Bri here to this time as well. I'm sorry for thinking ye mad. I dinna know any of that until Mother told me."

"Ah, I see. Well, I'm glad that you don't think I'm crazy."

"So tell me, lass. Tell me what all of those things are that ye spoke of."

Truly sleepy now, I found it hard to keep my eyelids open. I started to speak, but the words came out in between yawns. "Tomorrow, I'll tell you in the morning."

I allowed my head to roll to the side as I started to drift into sleep, but it took longer for sleep to find me than Baodan realized. I know he wouldn't have said what he did if he knew I could hear.

As I leaned into him, he bent downward to plant a kiss on the side of my head. "Aye, I shall happily wait until tomorrow to hear it. For every strange thing that ye utter from that beautiful mouth of yers is a pleasure to hear."

Chapter 14

Ach, trouble found him. The lass slept soundly against him, and she made the most unusual sounds in her sleep. The sweetest, softest coos of comfort that made his position on his horse so uncomfortable he found himself immensely grateful that she wasn't awake to know what she did to him. Each unconscious shift she made in front of him tempted him to slide his fingers up her thighs.

He shook his head to clear it. Seeing that the sun rose in the distance, he slowed Artair's pace so that he could find a suitable place for them to stop and rest. Temptation was a downfall of being a man, he supposed. No matter that he was no longer capable of love, it didn't stop his body from betraying him at the sight of a beautiful woman, and beautiful she was.

He'd never seen hair like hers, so red, curly and endless. A man could get lost in it, and he wished that he could do just that; to tug hard on it whilst he buried himself inside her.

He leaned down to smell of it, and his stomach grew taut from the sensation that washed over him. What sort of oils and creations must she have access to in her own time to make hair smell so wonderful?

And her eyes, he couldn't see them now, but they were eyes of such rarity that he need only see them once to remember them forever. They were the oddest combination of green and brown, each color so different and vibrant that from afar it looked as if her left eye was completely green and her right eye brown. In truth, at closer view, each eye had colors of both, and they were captivating and magical. They looked to him like the eyes that should be found in that of a mystical creature, not in an ordinary human.

Not that she was ordinary, she was anything but. Mitsy was loud, bold and, whether she intended to be or not, he found her quite amusing. He wanted to know more about her, more about her time and what had led her here. He hoped he wouldn't feel the need to sleep too long so that he could spend the day talking with her.

"Are ye ready to wake, lass? Artair here needs to rest, and I'll no deny that I do as well."

She threw her arms up to stretch sending one of her hands right into his jaw. She instantly swirled around to face him, an apology mixed with a not-so-subtle hint of amusement dancing in her eyes. "Oh, I'm sorry." She laughed and reached up to rub his jaw. "Does it hurt?"

He enjoyed the feeling of her hands on him. While it hadn't really hurt him at all, he was no fool. "Aye, it does, lass. Ye have a strong hand."

She glanced up at him knowingly, and his face warmed at the embarrassment of being found out.

"Well, here." She stretched upward and planted a brief kiss on his jawline. "All better?" Every muscle in his body went rigid. "What was that for?"

She shrugged as she continued to look over her shoulder at him. "It's just something that you do. Kiss a boo-boo to make it better. I don't know. Sorry, guess that trend hasn't caught on yet."

"Ah, well I know that ye doona know it, but ye stretch while ye sleep. Ye hit me then as well. Many times."

She grinned at him and laughed, turning quickly around

to face the front.

What had gotten into him? He was jesting her and it would only lead to trouble for them both.

* * *

I couldn't believe he'd actually ridden through the entire night. I knew that's what I told him to do, but he'd been dead on his feet after traveling. I expected him to ride until I fell asleep and then stop to make camp.

Instead, when he woke me at dawn, we were surrounded by landscape I would not have recognized from later centuries. I was immediately grateful he'd seen me fleeing from the castle. While I would probably have been able to find my way to Conall Castle during my own time, there were currently no roads or landmarks to help me find my way. Each tree looked much like the last.

He'd flirted with me, whether it had been his intention to do so or not. I supposed I gave him reason to though when I kissed him on the jaw, but it just seemed like too good of an opportunity to pass up. Any straight woman with normal levels of sex hormones would find their eggs quivering at the sight of my roadside companion.

As the horse came to a stop at Baodan's chosen place of rest, I slipped off the side of the horse, rather unthinkingly. I didn't take into account how numb my bottom would be, having grown so sore and numb that I couldn't feel it at all. As soon as my feet hit the ground, my knees buckled.

Before I could stand, Baodan lifted me up by both elbows, my chest grazing his as he did so. If my bum hadn't felt as if a thousand pin pricks were being stuck into it as blood found its way back to my rear, I would've found the touch quite flustering.

"Holy mother of crap! My ass hurts!"

Baodan looked down at me and laughed. "Ye have a penchant for swearing, doona ye? And ye are no accustomed to riding, or yer backside wouldna hurt ye so."

He let go now that I had my footing and twisted to stretch, which emphasized every chiseled muscle in his stomach.

"Although, I'm a wee bit sore meself. 'Twas a long ride."

I attempted to move around a bit, stretching and turning as much as the dress would allow, so that he wouldn't see me staring at him with awe. "I'm sorry. I shouldn't have made you ride all night. You have to rest now. I'll keep myself busy with something."

He looked as if he could fall over at any moment. I wasn't surprised that after riding all night, his need for sleep now outweighed his curiosity of finding out what happened to me the night before. "I'm sure ye will, lass. Ye doona seem like the sort of person to sit idly. Just stay close and doona get yerself into trouble, aye?"

I rolled my eyes and turned to walk a few trees down while he settled against the trunk next to the tree where he'd tied his horse. "Yes, sir. Sweet dreams."

He didn't answer and I looked back to see that his eyes were already closed. It seemed that I had at least a few hours to kill before we would move again, which was fine. I was eager to make it to Conall Castle, but my legs were none too eager to get back on a horse.

My stomach growled, and I looked around miserably at the vast emptiness. I'd never in my life appreciated the heart-clogging goodness of any fast-food restaurant the way I did in the moment. I'd not had time to think about food when I'd fled, and I expected that since Baodan hadn't intended to leave on another journey seconds after arriving home that he had little in the way of food with him.

He would be forced to hunt or gather something because Lord knew I didn't know how to do it. I couldn't stand the thought of being totally useless though. So as I marched around the wilderness, an idea of how I could help came to mind.

As a small child, I lived in an endless bounce of foster homes until I found Lilly. To be honest, I didn't remember much about most of them. It was a dark, lonely existence, and each time I entered a new home, I knew it would only be for a short period.

I did, however, remember one family very well. They'd been kind enough, but their real children never took to me. In the end, it just didn't work out. They were big into camping and we went often. I hated most of it, but I loved watching the dad build a fire. He created it the old-fashioned way with kindling and wood, said he learned it in Boy Scouts.

I'd been far too little at the time to try, but it occurred to me that perhaps I could give it a try now. Unless all Baodan gathered was berries, we would need to build a fire at some point. I could go ahead and get it started for him because there was no way in hell that I would eat raw meat. Hopefully by the time I gathered some kindling and found wood that would work, he would be rested enough to wake up and get me some food.

It took me a long time to find enough small branches and kindling to make anything work, but eventually I thought I had enough adequate materials to give it a go. I sat down to the task at hand and got to work, very quickly realizing what a complete and utter idiot I was.

I clearly missed some part of the equation because no matter how fast I ran my fingers up and down the pointed stick, not even a smidge of smoke rose out of the small pile. I got a little carried away with it though, and I continued to twirl my hands up and down the stick until my palms were red, only stopping at the sound of a stranger's voice behind me.

"Do ye need some help there, lass? Ye are no going to build a fire that way."

I turned to see a rather wild looking man make his way toward me. He had no horse, and it appeared as if he had traveled for some time. More than that really, he looked as if his home was amongst the trees. His hair a tangled mess, I could smell him as he approached, but he seemed harmless enough.

Maybe the stranger could help me get the fire started and then take his leave before Baodan woke, then I could impress him with my fire skills. "Yes, please. I'm afraid I really don't know what I'm doing."

"Aye, I can see that. Hand me that wee stick that yer holding."

He crouched down beside me, and I extended it in his direction as he pulled out a dirk and went to work on the stick, slowly shaping it into a much more pronounced point. Once he finished, he completely rearranged my pile and then moved to stand behind me. "It should be easier now, lass. Place yer hands back the way ye had them."

I did and he crouched down and hesitated. I turned around to smile at him. "It's ok. You can show me."

He grinned a nearly toothless smile and scooted closer so that he could wrap his arms around my back as he placed his hands over my own. Together we spun the stick. Just as smoke started to build at its base, Baodan's voice boomed through the trees.

"I would appreciate it, sir, if ye would take yer hands off me wife."

Chapter 15

Eoghanan hoped to capture the alchemist and secure him inside the dungeons quickly enough so that he could be back outside Mitsy's door by morning. It proved impossible. While he secured the man easily enough, he had to sneak him into the dungeon and, despite the man's small stature, he'd struggled to move his unconscious prisoner down that many stairs.

By the time the alchemist was inside a cell and regained consciousness, most of the morning passed. Every moment Eoghanan spent away from Mitsy's door, his worry grew for her. He needed to protect her, but he also needed to protect his family from the danger that lived among them. He looked up at the small window near the top of the cell. Seeing that the sun was past its midpoint, he decided now was his best time to move.

Niall should be out for his daily ride, which meant there would be a few precious moments to search for the poison to present to his prisoner. Surely if he showed the man his own vial, the alchemist would not be able to deny that he made the potion.

Once he acquired the poison, Eoghanan would check in on Mitsy. He would make certain that she'd been fed and, if he must, spend a few moments speaking with her in the hopes of lifting her spirits. Not that it would be an unpleasant task. He found the lass' company rather pleasing.

Surely Baodan would return today so that he could see the

lass safely to Conall Castle. With both of them gone, he would be free to resume his questioning of the man sitting in front of him without distraction.

Eoghanan shoved a glass of water in the alchemist's direction. "There is something that I must see to. I shall be back to visit with ye shortly. I doona wish ye harm, but I will have the truth from ye. If ye doona wish to give it freely, ye will leave me no choice but to hurt ye. Think on that whilst I am away."

The man called out to him as he started to leave causing Eoghanan to pause and face him.

"What is it that ye think I have done, sir, for I swear to ye there is nothing?"

"Ye have provided a man with a poison of much harm."

"Do ye have this poison that ye speak of? For I am no a maker of such potions."

"I doona now, but I will." Egohanan turned and left, praying with each footstep that his brother's room would be empty and Mitsy would be safe and sound in her own.

* * *

He held his breath as he opened his brother's door, only releasing it after finding the room vacant.

Once inside, he hurried as fast as he could, lifting every object in sight. He pulled open the window draping and as light streamed in, it bounced off of something beneath the bed. Crouching low, he saw the vial standing neatly underneath where his louse of a brother slept.

Niall would notice the poison's disappearance, but at this point, what did it matter? In a matter of days Eoghanan would reveal all of his brother's wrongs.

Slipping the vial safely away, he crept out of Niall's room, rounding the corner quickly in his hurry to check in on Mitsy. His heart froze at the sight of the bedchamber door hanging open and the only person standing inside the room was Rhona.

* * *

"What has happened here? Did I no tell ye to keep her inside?" He grabbed the old woman by both arms, shaking her as panic coursed through him.

She said nothing and he stopped as he noticed how she trembled, and he knew it wasn't from fear. Rhona feared no one. Releasing his grip, he directed her to a chair. "What is it, Rhona? Are ye all right?"

After fanning herself, she looked up at him in confusion. "Would ye believe me if I told ye I dinna know for certain? It seems that most of the castle fell suddenly verra ill during the night. I couldna see in front of me, and I grew too weak to get up off me knees. The guards outside the room said the same happened to them."

Niall. It had to be Niall. He felt the same way on the night of Osla's death, and his mother felt much the same way for months. "What happened to the lass that was in here, Rhona? Where's Mitsy?"

She shook her head. "I must have fallen asleep in the midst of me illness for when I awoke, Niall sat beside me. He told me that Baodan returned home and took the lass immediately for Conall Castle."

Rhona was no fool. Unlike most, he knew she didn't fall for Niall's charms. She'd always been suspicious of him. "Do ye believe him, Rhona? Did Baodan come here?"

She shook her head as she looked down at the floor regretfully. "No. I doona think that Baodan would have left so quickly with her. At the verra least, he would have spoken to me before he went. 'Twas clear that Niall had no been struck by the same illness as the rest of us, and I have no seen him or the lass since. When he spoke with me, I still couldna move, and he left me quickly."

"Did he take her, do ye think?" Surely, Niall would have no reason to and, if he had, he doubted the lass was still alive now.

"I doona think so. He seemed verra angry, and he walked with a bad limp. If he tried to capture the lass, I believe he failed to do so."

"Good." He turned to leave, his mind racing with all that he knew he must do. "Do ye know where he went?"

"No. I expect to the village. 'Tis where he likes to find all his lassies, and he seemed in a bad way. I expect he's gone in search of someone to soothe him. I hope that he willna, but I feel sure he shall."

"I have to go, Rhona. Will ye be all right here?"

He ran as she waved him on, back down to the dungeons. If Niall no longer stayed at the castle where he could keep an eye on him, it was more urgent than ever for him to gather the proof that he needed. His prisoner would give him answers tonight.

* * *

"Dammit man, I doona wish to hurt ye, but if ye doona tell me what ye know of this, ye will leave me no choice." Eoghanan extended the man a drink of water. He'd not laid a hand on him as of yet, and he hoped he wouldn't have to.

"Have I hurt ye yet? I doona mean ye harm, but I believe ye have been forced to provide a man something that has harmed others, aye?"

"Ye did hurt me. Ye hurt me head." Slowly the alchemist drank the water, staring back at Eoghanan with dismay.

"Would ye have come with me willingly?"

"No."

"Help me, sir. I have told ye I willna hurt ye unless I must. What are ye so afraid of?"

For the first time in days, a spark lit the man's eyes. "How can ye ask that? I have done nothing, but ye have locked me up like a criminal. If ye doona mean me harm, then why have ye brought me here?"

Why did he believe the man? No other held such a knowledge of herbs in the village. Of course, he knew his brother to be smart enough to think of looking elsewhere than his own village for the poison. It wouldn't do for people to learn the truth about him.

Eoghanan crouched down in front of his prisoner, regret in his heart for the injustice he now believed he'd done. "All right, lad, What are ye called? I'll tell ye the truth of what has happened, and ye must swear to do the same with me. For if I find later that ye have betrayed me and it was ye that he worked with, I can assure ye that I shall be the last one to see ye alive."

"Aye, I swear it. I have no reason to lie to ye. Me name is Durell."

"Fine. I believe that me brother acquired a poison and uses it to slowly poison our mother. 'Tis no the first time he used such a substance on another. She is gone from the castle now, so I have hope that she will heal, but she is still in danger

107

until I can prove his guilt."

The man looked horrified at the thought. He didn't provide the poison. "Surely, the laird couldna do such a thing. Why?"

Eoghanan shook his head, astonished at the man's conclusion. "No, 'twas no Baodan. 'Twas Niall. Now, I believe ye when ye say ye dinna aid him in this. Are there others who could have done so? Here is the poison that I spoke of before." He handed it to the man and watched as he stared at it.

Eoghanan held his breath while he waited.

Finally, Durell spoke. "Aye, I know who made this poison. There is a woman who lives no far from the village. She is no much of a healer. Only those who wish to bring foul things upon another seek her mixtures."

Eoghanan clasped the man on the shoulder, hopeful for the first time in many days. "Is there an antidote for this?" He knew this vial would not be the only one in Niall's possession. For him to have poisoned their mother for so long, he must have much more locked away.

"Aye, I can make ye one, but I shall need to be at me home with me herbs and mixtures."

Just as well, he needed to get to the village to find his brother anyway. If he found Niall and he did have Mitsy, or if he learned he'd harmed her, Eoghanan would not wait to gather proof. He would gladly kill his brother on the spot. "Verra well, we shall leave at once." He smiled at the look of relief on the old man's face. "I told ye I wouldna hurt ye and me apologies for yer head."

Chapter 16

The man released his grip on me immediately and jumped away like someone struck by lightning. "I'm verra sorry, sir," he told Baodan. "I was only trying to help her with the fire. I shall take me leave at once."

I stood up and held up a hand to stop him. "No, wait. Thank you. I needed your help. Stay and have a meal with us before you leave. You stay and get the fire started and my *husband*," I couldn't help but say the word sarcastically, "and I will go in search of some food."

"Only if yer husband finds this acceptable." He looked down at his feet, clearly intimidated by Baodan.

I walked over to Baodan and grabbed him firmly by the hand so that I could drag him off to where he had left his horse.

"He insists upon it. We will be back in a little while with something to eat."

I squeezed Baodan's hand as tightly as I could, but I knew it didn't cause him the pain that I'd hoped. Once we were out of earshot, I turned on him. "Are you crazy? What the hell is the matter with you?"

"Me?" He genuinely looked shocked. "Ye're the one who allowed that vagabond to lay hands on ye, lass. He could have dirked ye right in the side, and ye would have been helpless to stop him."

"He was just helping me. I tried to start a fire to help you out, and I didn't have the slightest idea what I was doing, but all of that is beside the point. Why did you tell him I was your wife?"

"It isna suitable for ye to be traveling alone with a man who isna yer husband."

"But I am traveling with someone who isn't my husband. Do you really think that man cares about what is suitable or not?"

"I doona care what he thinks, lass, but until we get to Conall Castle, ye shall be seen as me wife to anyone we may cross paths with. Now," he reached out and grabbed me by the wrist, dragging me behind him as he traveled farther away from the man and our fire. "Ye have promised this man food to eat, and food we shall give him."

* * *

Lots of daylight remained by the time we finished eating. We could have traveled a good distance further but our wild man, who later introduced himself as Alec, seemed starved for conversation and chatted our ears off until sundown.

It turned out Baodan was far less of a hard ass than he tried to make himself appear, for it didn't take long before he softened to Alec. By the end of the evening, he offered Alec work at MacMillan Castle if wished it.

After hours of listening to the two men talk, I zoned out until Baodan's touch on my hand drew me out of my daze. "I'm sorry. What did you say?"

"Alec just said that we make a handsome couple, and I told him 'twas only because of me wife's beauty."

He winked at me playfully, and I rolled my eyes.

Alec stood and smiled in our direction. "Aye, it has done

me heart good to witness two people so truly in love. Gives me hope that I may one day find a lassie of me own." He tore his gaze away from me to address Baodan. "Why doona ye just kiss her already? I can see in yer eyes that ye wished to do so all afternoon, but ye have been denied the pleasure of doing so by me presence. Go on and do it now. 'Tis been too long since I've seen a proper kiss."

I stilled where I sat, but Baodan stood in a moment, yanking me up so that I pressed flush against him.

"Aye lad, if ye wish to see a kiss, I am in no mood to deny ye."

It was rough and consuming, the way his lips met mine. There was a heat in his lips, a passion that had been suppressed for far too long, and I was more than happy to help sate it. He had one hand woven into my hair, gripping the back of my neck so tightly I could only move my lips in response to him when he allowed it. With his other hand against the smallest part of my lower back, he pressed himself into me. I could feel his heart beating rapidly in his chest.

He had yet to break for air, and I worried he would pass out from the effort. He kissed like a man too long without love. While possibly less practiced than his younger brother, he made up for it in talent.

I didn't care that Alec watched, but I found myself wishing he wasn't there. Maybe if we were alone I could've persuaded him to just rip all of my clothes off and take me right by the fire.

When I could take no more or pass out myself, I reached up with my right hand and pressed it lightly on his face. He stilled and I realized in that instant that he'd lost himself. It broke my heart to be the one to pull him back to reality. I got the feeling that he didn't often allow such weakness in himself.

An apology lay behind his eyes, and I reached up to kiss him lightly in the hopes that he would know it was okay. How could it not be? There wasn't a woman alive who would have been bothered by that kiss.

To the left of us, Alec started clapping and I blushed as Baodan released his grip on my neck. Pulling away so that our chests no longer touched, we both moved so that we faced each other once more, but Baodan kept his arm around me, holding me tightly in the crook of his arm.

"I couldna have dreamed up a kiss as wonderful as that. Well done. Now 'tis time for me to take leave of ye both and find camp for the night. Thank ye both for yer kindness."

He turned to leave, but Baodan spoke to stop him. "'Tis already dark and I doona wish to ride at night again. Why doona ye set camp here with us tonight, and we may take our leave of one another in the morning?"

Alec nodded and went about the business of rolling out his small blanket for sleeping. I knew he had to be relieved not to travel elsewhere after dark, but I suspected that Baodan aasked him to stay for another reason.

If someone else camped with us, Baodan would insist that we share where we lay our heads to sleep. For in the company of others, we had to maintain the façade of being husband and wife.

Chapter 17

We had only one blanket and spread it out over the ground for us both to lay on. Though a warm evening, the wind chilled enough to cause me to shiver despite the nearness of him. I lay with my back against his chest. Neither of us spoke until we heard Alec snoring on the other side of the dwindling fire.

"Come here, lass. Turn into me."

I hesitated, but as a breeze whipped through the trees, I trembled and rolled over to face him. He removed a pin from his kilt and held a large portion of it over me like a cape. Thank God the kilt had enough fabric to keep him covered for I knew I wouldn't be able to refrain from taking a looksee if it hadn't.

I scooted until I was up against him and he could envelope me under part of his kilt. I glanced up at the dark sky to clear my head. The idea that I basically lay inside his clothes with him filled my head with impure thoughts.

Eventually, I let out a breath. With it, I realized how tense I really was. Why? I was in no danger here with him. In fact, I felt more protected than I had in ages. I pulled my eyes down from the sky to look at him. "Why did you do that?"

He reached up with his hand to brush a lock of hair from my face. "Do what, lass?"

"Suggest that he camp here with us."

"Ye doona think that I did it so that the poor lad wouldna have to find a place to set camp after dark?"

"No."

"I think 'twas only that I wanted to be near ye. Do ye mind lass? He's asleep now. If ye wish to sleep on yer own, ye can."

I opened my hands that were balled against his chest to lay them flat against him so he wouldn't move. "No, I don't mind."

He leaned forward and kissed me on the forehead. "Good. Now," he scooted away just a tad so that he could look at me more clearly. "'Tis past time that ye tell me what happened back at the castle to upset ye so and caused ye to leave before I returned for ye."

I grimaced at the thought of it. There'd been enough activity today to distract me from thinking of the unfortunate incident. "Fine, but you have to promise that you'll take me to Conall Castle. No matter what I tell you, you can't decide to turn around and head back home."

He continued to stroke my hair. "Was it really that bad? Please tell me that he dinna hurt ye. He only said something to upset ye, aye?"

I shook my head but spoke quickly to clarify. "No, he didn't hurt me. I'm fine. I did however, hurt him quite badly."

His eyes widened in surprise, but he said nothing so that I would continue. "Promise first. Promise that you'll take me to Conall Castle."

He nodded but worry filled his face. "Aye, fine lass, I promise, but spit it out."

I didn't want to re-hash the whole incident so I spoke quickly, just giving him the highlights. I knew he would need nothing more to get spitfire angry. "He got into the room and tried to buy me. He threw a bag of change down on the table. Although I told him I wasn't what he thought, he planned to receive what he believed he'd purchased."

Baodan's hand stopped on my hair. Even in the moonlight, I could see his face grow pale.

"He didn't touch me. I tried to take advantage of the situation and convinced him to take his clothes off first. He did and, once he was on top of me, well, I…" I found it difficult to finish. I knew he would rear back in disgust. Although I believed it had been necessary, I could hardly believe I'd done it myself.

"What did ye do, lass? Did ye kill him?"

I sat up, taken aback by his assumption. "What? No! Of course I didn't kill him."

He seemed to breathe a sigh of relief but pulled me close to him again and reached up to soothe me once more. "Well, if ye had, there was just cause for ye to do so. If ye dinna kill him, what did ye do?"

"I yanked on his junk so hard he passed out."

He pulled away and sat up on his elbow so that he could look down on me. "His 'junk'?"

I tried to gesture with my hands, but it just looked ridiculous. "You know…his balls and his…I don't know what you call it here, his baby maker."

A brief moment of silence followed, but he could no longer contain himself, and he erupted into the most ridiculous and inappropriate fit of laughter I ever heard.

I moved from beneath his kilt and sat with my legs crossed in front of him, staring down disapprovingly. "How is that even the littlest bit funny? If it hadn't worked, he probably would have killed me!"

He reached out to try and grab me in between hoots of laughter but I jerked away, suddenly angry. Eventually, he pulled himself together and sat up in front of me looking guilty.

"I'm sorry, lass, truly."

"Why were you laughing at that? It's not funny. It was downright terrifying, and I probably did some serious damage to him."

"'Tis no funny at all what he tried to do to ye and, believe me, Eoghanan shall no be welcome inside McMillan Castle after I return, brother or no. I only laugh because I havena ever in me life heard of a man's dobber and bawz referred to as ye did."

I laughed at his reference to the male anatomy. It sounded no less odd than my own to me, but I tensed suddenly as I registered the name he'd just uttered. "Wait! Did you just say E-o, I mean Eoghanan?"

"Aye, lass. I willna have him in the castle after what he did to ye."

"But it wasn't Eoghanan. It was Niall."

He shifted, uncomfortably. "What did ye just say?"

"You heard what I said. Eoghanan showed me nothing but kindness. Niall did it, the disgusting creep." Baodan looked as if I'd slapped him. "What's wrong?"

He quieted for a moment, then shook his head somberly while he spoke. "I'm ashamed of meself, lass, for assuming it was Eoghanan. He is many things, but he is no a man who would try to force himself on a lass."

"And Niall is?"

"I have never known him to use force, but he doesna treat women the way they deserve. While I am no too pleased with Eoghanan either, I feel me assumption to be a betrayal of the man I know he is." He lay down once more and held the longest part of his kilt out for me again. "Come back here. I am in awe of ye."

"You're in awe?" It hardly seemed an appropriate emotion for the current situation. "Why?"

"Aye, I am. I have never heard of a woman denying him. 'Tis why he tried to force himself I'm sure, and ye dinna only deny him, ye gave him no less than he deserved. I am proud of ye."

"Well...thanks." I could scarcely stay mad at him for laughing when he'd clearly meant all that he said to be a compliment.

I'd yet to join him back under his kilt, and he waved the edge around like a cape. It looked ridiculous. "Am I forgiven? If so, come and join me here again."

"For laughing? Aye." I smiled as he shook his head at my attempt to mimic his accent and moved to snuggle in close to him again. My cheek pressed against his bare chest and his chin rested on the top of my head. "What did Eoghanan do to you? What were you two talking about the day I arrived here?"

He didn't move away from me, but his chest gave as he let out a large breath. "'Tis no a happy story."

I reached up to trail my fingertips down his arm in the hopes that it would soothe him. I didn't wish to anger him, I only wanted to know more about the history between them. "I don't always need stories to be happy. I have quite a few unhappy ones of my own."

"I was married once, lass."

"Once?" So this was the "her" they spoke of.

"Aye and 'tis a long story, lass, and I find meself suddenly sleepy. Perhaps I may tell ye another time."

His heart beat even more quickly than mine and, despite

the sadness in his voice at the memory of whatever he hesitated to tell me, the sexual tension was so palpable, I knew he didn't really think I would believe him sleepy. "You're not about to fall asleep and you have all night to tell it, but you don't have to if you're not comfortable."

He kissed the top of my head but held me close. As much for his own comfort as mine.

"It was no for verra long. Something forced me to leave her for a few days to assist a man from the village, and I left her in Eoghanan's care while I was away. When I returned, I found her dead."

"How?" The wind seemed suddenly even colder.

"A - a sickness."

He tried to hide it but I saw how he hesitated. I didn't know him well and, he was under no obligation to tell me, but I knew there was more to the story than he said. For while it went a ways to explaining Baodan's feelings toward his brother, it still didn't make much sense to me. If she really passed of a sickness, how was that Eoghanan's fault? Chances were, Baodan would have been no more help to her than his brother.

"I'm sorry." I felt the knot he swallowed and regretted asking the question.

I pulled away so that I could look at his eyes. They were cold and hard, different from how I'd ever seen them. This part of his past he spent every moment trying to bury within him.

"I'm sorry," I repeated myself, and the words sounded silly and useless. What good were they to him now? But I didn't know what else to say.

"Doona be. 'Twas many years ago. I only regret I wasna there to save her, for the guilt of that has turned me into someone verra hard."

"Hard?" I found him anything but. I thought him kind, funny, and gentle.

"Aye. I doona feel like I once did. I doona allow meself to. I enjoy friendship. It causes me hurt when others are in pain, but I doona care about others the way a man should."

"What does that mean? How should a man care about others? You were kind to me even though you thought me a lunatic when you found me. You offered Alec a place to stay and something to give him purpose. You didn't have to do that. I think you care more than most. You're a good man, Baodan."

"Thank ye, but that is no what I mean. I am no capable of love anymore, of caring for someone enough to allow them to care for me in return. I am hardened irreparably. Only fools allow such hurt into their lives because, in the end, all love is a hurt."

Not that I could prove him wrong from personal experience, but even I knew what he said to be total bullshit. I didn't think he even really believed it himself but I didn't want to argue with him, not when I initiated the conversation. He wouldn't have told me any of what he thought unless I had asked him.

Instead, I said nothing, snuggling into the warmness of him as I let sleep take me.

* * *

Sometime in the night, Baodan roused me by shaking me lightly on the shoulder and whispering in my ear. "I'm sorry to wake ye, but I canna sleep."

I stretched and, as I did so, the front of my body pushed

into him. I instantly had a pretty good idea of why he woke me. "I told you that you weren't about to fall asleep."

He grinned and scooted down on the blanket so that our heads were even. Reaching out with his left hand, he cupped the side of my face and pulled me close. I was wide awake now. His nose touched mine as he stared deep into my eyes. "What was it that ye called them, lass? 'Balls?'"

I laughed and nodded, the tip of my nose tickling the tip of his. "Yes. Why?"

"If I kiss ye again, will me balls be in danger? I doona wish to meet the same fate as me brother." He asked it slowly, his eyes teasing me as he brought his lips closer to mine only to pull them away just before they touched.

Slow torture, the tension between us, that made every limb in my body weak and fluttery with the anticipation of imagining his lips claiming mine once more. Our chests rose and fell quickly in a synced rhythm that pained me as if I ran at full speed.

I didn't answer him. There was no need. Instead I pressed my trembling lips against his and moved slowly against him. He grinned against my mouth, and I nudged his nose as I moved close to trace the center of his upper lip with my tongue.

He groaned and pushed his hips against me. Hard, ready, the solid length of him hurt me in a delicious way as it pressed into the fragile bone protecting my center.

I returned each kiss full force, content to relish in the pleasure of exploring one another until sunrise if he wished it. But as he trailed my face and neck and chest with his lips, I quickly realized that, despite the condition he found himself in, he had no intention of undressing me. He focused all of his attention upward, on kissing me in such a way that each breath I took was not my own but a breath given to me by him as he took claim on my mouth. That in and of itself proved to me just how capable he was of caring.

After his confession, he would think that to sleep with me would make him no better than his brothers. To show respect for me in such a way negated everything that he believed about himself.

For any man incapable of love would not have been so considerate, so selfless.

Chapter 18

We left at sunrise, bidding Alec goodbye before beginning our final leg toward Conall Castle. We'd fallen asleep wrapped in one another's arms. While I glowed from the make-out session fit to rival the horniest of teenagers, Baodan seemed a little worse for wear.

It wasn't good for a man to be that ready for that long and do nothing about it. I'd have been happy to help provide him some release, but with his strict and warped perception of himself, it would have tortured him to do more.

He remained quiet all morning, but I didn't care. I expected he wrestled with what he knew to be true. He did care and, whether I wanted to admit it or not, so did I.

Lost in thought when he nudged me, he pointed out in front at the stone façade in the distance. "We are almost there, lass. Ye will finally be able to see yer Bri."

I threw my hands up in the air, and he laughed in my ear. "Yay! She's going to freak out! Do you think she knows I'm coming?"

"I doona know. I would say no, but if the witch could send ye through time, I suppose she could warn Bri of yer arrival, aye?"

"Yes, I'm sure she could. I hope that she hasn't though. I would like to surprise her." He slowed Artair and turned him off of our trail. "What are you doing?"

"Do ye mind if we stop just a moment, lass? I need to move me legs a bit."

* * *

He didn't want to get to the castle. Once they were there, he would scarcely see her. He would speak with Bri's supposed twin, Blaire, for a bit and stay the evening but then he would have no reason to stay, and he couldn't bear the thought of leaving Mitsy.

He tried to tell himself that he only worried for her safety, but he knew he lied to himself. She would be safer with his cousins than she would be in his own home, for his brothers didn't live with the Conalls.

Last night had him out of sorts with all that he knew about himself. He'd not experienced joy like that he felt at holding her through the night in many years, but it had also been the worst sort of torture.

Every instant his mouth met hers, he yearned to lift her dress so that he could thrust himself deep inside her. He wished to hear her cry out in response to him and for her to clench around him as he came inside her.

It wasn't that he'd not been with women since the death of his wife. He found release with many, but it had been different. He'd not given them promises like his brother, not deflowered virgins or bought whores. He found women much like himself who lost loves and didn't want another. They each sought the same as him, a night of companionship to shut out the loneliness that encompassed their lives.

There should've been no reason for him to refrain from lying with her if she allowed it. He told her the truth, just as he had to all the other women, but to then claim her would have been to put her aside with all the rest. He couldn't bring himself to do that.

He lied to everyone about the true nature of his wife's death, but when he uttered the lie to Mitsy, his stomach grew ill. She was different. She deserved better, someone who could give her every piece of his soul, not someone who lied to protect himself from speaking of a painful memory.

As much as he wished he could be that person, he didn't have enough left in him to give. He knew once they got to Conall Castle, whether she decided to stay in this time or return to her own, he would lose her, and he wished to kiss her just once more.

Once Artair stopped, Baodan dismounted quickly, turning to help her down before taking off into the trees. He heard her call out to him, but he didn't turn around until she caught up to him and reached out to grab his hand.

"Hey, what's wrong with you? Where are you going so fast?"

He spun and pushed her hard against the trunk of the nearest tree, crushing himself against her. To be near her frightened him more than anything in the world. After this kiss, he wouldn't allow himself to be so scared ever again.

Her lips were soft, warm, and sweet; everything that he was not. Abruptly she pulled away, and he forced himself to close off the dream of her.

He stepped back and looked down. There were words written in her eyes, something she wished to say but hesitated to do so.

He squeezed her hand to encourage her. "What is it, lass? I like the way ye say all the things that enter yer mind. Doona stop now."

"That isn't the kiss of someone who doesn't care. Believe me, I've had them. Men who don't care don't kiss someone like that."

She let go and started walking back to Artair. It would be too cruel to allow her to hope. "Mitsy, lass, ye are wrong. 'Twas no the kiss of a caring man. 'Twas the kiss of a man who's been too long without a woman."

His throat burned at the lie that even he couldn't believe. She faced him, her expression giving nothing away. As always, she didn't mince her words.

"Then don't ever kiss me again because if you mean it, I deserve far better than you."

It hurt him to his very soul just how right she was.

Chapter 19

What a moron. I truly didn't think that he even believed himself what he said. Even so, any man should know better than to say something like that out loud to a woman, even if he thought it. It was like saying that he used me, but his actions had shown otherwise.

His words didn't hurt my feelings, they just pissed me off. I just couldn't understand his mindset. It was terrible that he'd been hurt, but if he thought no one else had ever had love bite them in the ass, he was delusional.

Maybe I was just a serial optimist. All of the modern conveniences that I had the pleasure of using throughout my life aside, I knew I had a harder life than him. He was a Scottish laird who grew up in a castle, for goodness sake. He had a mother and father who loved him. He'd never been poor.

I was an orphan who spent my childhood without family and with only one close friend. I'd not been born into a family filled with love, and I'd be paying off student loan debt for the rest of my life. I'd been burnt by love more than a few times myself, but never for a moment had I thought about just shutting myself off from all feelings or emotions.

His cowardice disappointed me, but I refused to let him put a damper on my day. I hadn't seen Bri in over a year. I couldn't wait to squeeze her neck and catch up.

The rest of the ride remained silent and awkward after the incident in the woods, but thankfully we were close to Conall Castle. As we approached the castle's stables, there seemed to be few people about. I worried for a moment that perhaps they wouldn't be home.

Baodan approached the stables and called out to who I assumed was the stable master. "Kip? Are ye in there?"

Inside the stalls, I knew the voice who answered us, and it wasn't the Kip that Baodan called out to. I recognized it instantly as that of Bri's look-a-like, Blaire.

"Is that ye, Baodan? What are ye doing..." she paused as she popped her head up out of the last stall and looked at me.

I could only hope Bri's face would look half as surprised. I waved as I spoke to her. "Don't worry. I won't attack you this time."

Baodan dismounted from the horse, and looked up at me in utter bewilderment. "Do ye know her, lass? That isna Bri, ye know."

Blaire stepped out of the stall and made her way quickly over to Baodan, wrapping her arms around him as if he were her long lost brother. "Aye, she knows I'm no Bri. We've met before."

"How?"

Baodan reached up to help me off the horse, but I wouldn't take his hand. Instead flipping over so that my belly touched the horse's back, I slid off onto the ground.

Once I grounded myself, Blaire pulled away from Baodan and moved to give me a hesitant hug before stepping away. She remained skittish around me. Not that I could blame her. The first time I saw her, I'd mistaken her for Bri. I thought Bri pretended to be someone else and it made me so angry, I'd attacked her in one of my most regrettable ginger moments.

Blaire reached out to touch Baodan's arm. "Ach, I forgot that ye dinna know. Before we were engaged, I'd been living forward in time. In the same time that Bri and Mitsy here come from."

That was news to me. It was my turn to look bewildered. "What? You two were engaged?"

Baodan shook his head and started to move Artair into an empty stall. "Long story, and one that doesna need to be told. Blaire, will ye take Mitsy to her?"

She reached out for my arm and together we left the stables. "Aye, o'course. I was only tending to the new colt here. I'll send Eoin and Arran out for ye, and they'll see ye inside once ye've seen to yer horse."

As we left Baodan, Blaire pointed up to a high window near the top of the castle. "I expect we will find her nursing the baby. I hope the wee thing isna sleeping. If she is, it willna be for long with the way Bri will scream at the sight of ye."

"Baby?"

She didn't answer, only nodded and grinned as she led me inside the castle.

* * *

We only just turned down the hallway that held the room where Blaire seemed to think Bri would be when I heard an American accent whisper quite loudly behind me.

"Oh my God! Mitsy!"

I turned to see Bri's mother, Adelle, walking toward me excitedly, a sleeping bundle wrapped in her arms. I smiled as I met her, shocked for the third time in a matter of minutes. "Adelle! What are you doing here? Is there anybody that Morna hasn't got her witchy claws on?"

"Oh, I guess you didn't come here on your own then did you, dear? Don't be too hard on Morna though, she knows what she's doing. She wouldn't have sent you here unless you needed to be here."

I reached over to embrace Adelle, making sure not to squish the sleeping babe. I lifted the blanket to get a better look at the beautiful dark-headed girl. I thought I might cry at the happiness I felt for Bri as I looked down at the small child. Bri always wanted nothing more than a family of her own. "She's beautiful. What a happy grandma you must be."

"Happy indeed, I'm even married myself now."

I'd never seen Adelle look so happy. The seventeenth century seemed to agree with the Montgomery women. "Get it, Adelle!" I winked at her, knowing she was as crass as me and wouldn't be offended. "Is he good to you?"

She chuckled once and then stopped so she wouldn't wake the baby. "Too good. I'm not worthy of him, but I don't plan on letting him go any time soon. Bri's in there." She pointed in the direction Blaire and I were headed. "I told her I'd get little Ellie asleep so that she could get a little nap in herself. Go in there and wake her up. She'll be so excited to see you, she'll think she's dreaming." She leaned forward and kissed me on the cheek before starting off down the hallway. "Love you, sweetie. We'll talk more later."

With Adelle gone, Blaire waved me over to the doorway and opened it just a crack before whispering in my direction. "There ye go. I'm off to find the lads."

I crept in to the room and walked over to the edge of the bed, grinning as I looked down at her. She slept as she always did, with her hands above her head and her mouth hanging wide open. It would've been kinder for me to allow her to sleep, but it also would have been totally out of character.

I gave her a light shake as I spoke. "Wake up, sleepy head. Turns out you're not as bat shit crazy as I thought. I really worried about you for a while."

Her eyelids flickered open slowly, and I laughed as I watched her eyes adjust. When they finally did, she all but tumbled out of the bed in her rush to stand so that she could look at me properly.

"Mitsy! Oh my gosh, I hoped you would come, but I wasn't sure if you ever would. Did you get the letter?"

She wrapped her arms around me in a hug so tight I could scarcely breathe. I patted her back in an effort to get her to release me, but she would only do so when she was good and ready. "I did find your letter. Let's sit down."

Eventually she let me go and crawled back on to the bed, motioning for me to join her.

We sat crisscross on the bed in front of one another. For a while, she just stared at me, smiling as if she thought she'd never see me again. And I suppose, she could've been right.

"Why did you leave the letter?" There'd been more to it than her just wanting to give me the option. She knew something, something that made her believe that things wouldn't work out with Brian.

Her smile faded, and I thought her eyes hinted of guilt.

"Why don't you tell me why you decided to come here first?"

"He cheated and did for most of our relationship, I think. Not that it was all his fault, I knew he was an asshole. He never really tried to hide that fact, but I married him anyway."

She nodded, knowingly. "Total asshole."

"Did you know, Bri? That he was cheating?"

"Not until the wedding. I…"

She hesitated and I didn't blame her for doing so. Who wanted to be the one to tell someone that the night of their wedding, their husband had been screwing another girl?

"It's fine, Bri. I don't care anymore. Really."

"I went in search of a restroom during the reception. With the women's being cleaned, the janitor directed me to one in a private office down the hallway. I heard him with a woman inside. I should've told you, but I couldn't bring myself to do it that night. That's why I left the letter. I figured when you found out about him yourself, you would know why I sent it. How long have things been bad?"

I shrugged. The real question was when were they ever not bad? "They always were. I think inside I knew he cheated, but I didn't find out about it until a few months ago."

"When did you get the letter?"

"Oh that. Brace yourself, I know you're going to blow a gasket. Brian gave that to me the day before I came here to Scotland. He'd opened it the week after the wedding. He stayed in your place with her."

Her eyes tripled in size. "That son of a bitch. Oh, if I was there I would have unleashed a whole barrel of crazy on his sorry ass. I'm so sorry. I didn't ever think...I wouldn't have..."

I grabbed her hand. "Of course you didn't think about that. Why would you? It's fine, I'm just glad he gave me the letter. I didn't believe a word inside it of course. I only came to Scotland because I believed you were in some sort of brainwashy cult."

She laughed and shifted her position on the bed. "What? I told you in Edinburgh. Although, I knew you didn't believe me."

"How could I? This is the craziest thing I've ever experienced." My own feet were asleep so I rolled off the side of the bed and moved about the room to stomp the tickle out of them.

"It is crazy, but amazing. I was always meant to be here, I think. What do you think about all of it?"

Many things ran through my mind: the blisters on my toes from uncomfortable shoes that rubbed, the lack of toilet paper, the miserable meals, no hot running water. "I think most of it is completely terrible. Parts of it though," Baodan crossed my mind, "aren't so bad."

"Parts huh?" She looked up at me knowingly. "You obviously didn't just end up here. Where did you land and who brought you here now?"

* * *

It wasn't his intention to listen in on the lassies' conversation. He'd been on his way to a room to rest and clean up after far too many days out of doors. The sound of his voice being uttered from Mitsy's lips stopped him cold.

"What do you know about him? Baodan?"

He pressed his back flat against the wall, only leaning his ear toward the doorway so that he could hear Bri's response.

"I don't know a lot, only that I like him very much. He's very close friends with Blaire, and she adores him. He has to be a pretty good guy to remain friends with someone who dumps him days before she's supposed to marry him."

He probably imagined it, but Mitsy's voice when she answered almost sounded jealous. "About that. How did that happen? Baodan told me yesterday that he isn't capable of loving anymore, whatever the hell that means. Why would he have asked her to marry him? Did they date or something? Do people do that here?"

Bri's voice was calm, a perfect counter to her fiery friend. With great insight, she seemed to understand his relationship with Blaire better than most.

"I don't think he ever loved Blaire. I think he enjoyed her friendship and wanted to help her when she was heartbroken and alone."

"Hmm…that sounds like something the silly fool would do."

He didn't know what she meant by that, but she was still clearly upset by what he'd said to her earlier.

"Oh, you've got it bad, don't you?"

Baodan couldn't repress a grin at Bri's question. While he didn't understand the exact meaning of it, he understood the connotation well enough. She asked if Mitsy fancied him.

"Why would you say that?"

"Oh, come on Mitsy. Your face is all red just from talking about him. And Mits…everyone is capable of love. If he took the time to tell you that he wasn't, he obviously likes you very much."

"Well, that's what I thought! But when I gave him the perfect opportunity to 'fess up, he was a total wuss."

He didn't know what that was, but was he really so transparent?

Quietly, he stepped away from the doorway but stopped at Bri's next question. The question he wanted to know the answer to since soon after he met her.

"What are you going to do? Will you stay here?"

Mitsy stood close to him, leaning against the wall he supposed, for her voice when she spoke sounded right next to him. He could offer nothing, but he wished with every fiber that she would stay.

"I expect I'll leave. I love you, Bri, but I couldn't stay here with you and your family. It wouldn't be right, and there's not much for a woman on her own to do around here."

He shouldn't have expected her to stay, but his heart felt like lead in his chest at the thought of her being centuries ahead of him. If she wanted to leave, it would be wrong of him to stop her.

He moved away from the door and made haste down the hallway. The castle walls suddenly restrained him. He needed to get outside to clear his head, to remind himself that he'd only known the lass a few short days.

* * *

Bri waited until his footsteps disappeared before she looked at me knowingly. "How long did you know he was standing on the other side of that door?"

I laughed, pleased with myself. "I heard him walking down the hallway before he ever stopped. You did too, right? Why did he think no one would notice the sudden lack of movement?"

Bri stood and moved to put her arm around me grinning. "Yes, I noticed. So you really don't have any intention of leaving, right? Please say you don't."

I reached up to pat her arm. "No, I'm not going to leave right away. I don't know if I'll stay forever, but if it's alright, I'd like to stay for a while. I have this magic rock that Morna gave me so I can go back to our own time whenever I want, but the truth is I have little to go back to. You and your mother are the closest thing I have to family. Until I figure out what it is I really want, I'd like to stay."

Bri squeezed me and stepped away so that she could point at the door. "Good! Now, go and find him and see how upset he is. If he has any sense, he'll talk you out of leaving. I expect you'll find him sitting out on the outer wall. He hung out there a lot when he was here caring for Blaire. I'll show you the way."

I hoped I hadn't made a mistake by lying, but I wanted to see if he would be bothered at the thought of me leaving. I suspected by his sudden disappearance from the doorway that he was, but I supposed I would find out for sure soon enough. "Was it wrong for me to do that?"

Bri looked over her shoulder at me as we walked down the hallway. "Not at all, girl. It was very well played."

Chapter 20

I found him where Bri expected, and it pleased me to see that he did look very upset about something. He glanced backward at me as I crawled out on the edge to sit beside him but said nothing.

"Thank you." I leaned in to him, just barely nudging my shoulder with his to get his attention.

He didn't turn to look at me, instead facing straight ahead as he spoke. "For what, lass?"

"For bringing me all the way here. You didn't have to."

His arms crossed and he appeared uncomfortable. "Aye, I did, lass. I couldna allow ye to travel alone."

He wasn't going to give me the answer I searched for, not without a little prying anyways. "And I suppose that's the only reason you brought me? You just couldn't stand the thought of me not being safe?"

"Aye. I did no less than any decent man would."

I crossed my own arms as I turned my body to stare at the side of his head. My temper flared and, if he didn't watch it, he would find himself on the receiving end of some serious ginger rage. It was unfair of him to be so cool toward me. "So, when you will return home?"

"At sunrise. I have responsibilities at home. I have been away for too long."

I couldn't believe that he planned on leaving so soon. I thought he would at least stay a few days. "Well," I could hardly utter the lie. "I guess this is goodbye then. I'm planning on returning home tonight."

"Aye? Well, safe journey to ye, lass."

About to cry, I didn't wish for him to see me do so. I spun myself around so that I could crawl off the ledge and re-enter the castle. He stared straight ahead, behaving as if my leaving was of no consequence to him.

Perhaps it had only been me who felt it, and our few days together seemed nothing unusual for him.

A sob bubbled up. While I tried to get away, I knew he heard me start to cry as I crawled back inside the main building. He did nothing to try to stop or comfort me. It seemed I was the wrong one. He told the truth before. He was incapable of feeling anything.

* * *

Why did he feel like crying? He never cried. Not once, since the death of his wife had he done so. He stared into the black sky in front of him, trying not to blink so that tears would dry in his eyes rather than fall.

Only the sound of Blaire's angry voice behind him pulled him from his trance.

"Baodan McMillan, if ye doona get yer arse off that wall and go after that lass, I shall kick ye off the edge and watch ye fall to the bottom."

"What are ye talking about, Blaire?" He spun and dropped himself back onto the walkway where Blaire stood.

"Doona do that. Ye know what I'm talking about. Ye are a fool. Ye care about her, doona ye?"

He couldn't lie to Blaire, not about this. She would never believe him even if he tried. "Aye, I do, but I doona know how to love someone anymore. I told ye that when I asked ye to marry me. I doona want it, and she deserves to spend her life with someone who can love her. That isna me."

"Are ye saying that I dinna deserve more than that?"

Ach, he didn't know how to speak to women. He only knew how to upset them. "No, o'course ye did. 'Tis only that I believed ye dinna want love either. Mitsy does, and she should have it."

Blaire shocked him by moving toward him and slapping him hard across the face. "Ye do want love, ye silly fool! I am going to say something to ye that I heard Adelle say once. It isna verra nice, and ye willna have heard it before, but I expect ye will understand the meaning well enough. Besides, I doona think kindness is what ye need right now."

His head spun from the impact of her hit. He had a hard head, but she had a strong hand. "Aye, say it. It canna be worse than ye knocking me upside me head."

"Doona be such a chicken shit! Ye say that ye doona know how to love so that ye doona ever have to hurt. 'Tis true that ye may be out of practice, but ye can learn, and she'd give ye the chance to do so."

He reached up to run his hands over his face. "I'm frightened that I willna be enough for her."

Blaire softened and reach out a hand to him. "Do ye remember what I told ye the day I ended our engagement?"

He shook his head. "Perhaps. Remind me."

"I told ye that one day ye'd find the person ye were meant to be with. Although ye told me ye dinna think it would happen, 'twas what ye said last that was important. Ye said that if such a love came, ye would welcome it."

Surely not; he couldn't imagine himself saying such a thing, but then again, Blaire always had a way of making him tell the truth. "And ye think that Mitsy is that love?"

"Aye, I do. I know that ye havena known her long, but she was meant to come to ye. I saw it."

He glanced suspiciously down at her. "What do ye mean by that? Have ye joined the lady Morna and taken up witchcraft?"

She elbowed him playfully in the side. "No, o'course I dinna, but I do believe that Morna showed me something. Do ye remember when Arran and I came to stay at McMillan Castle after leaving the castle formerly known as Kinnaird?"

He nodded. "Aye, I do. What of it?"

"As we left and rode by yer pond, I saw a red-head swimming in the water. I knew the lass looked just like Mitsy, but I thought at the time that I'd imagined it. I dinna make sense of the vision until ye both arrived here this afternoon. She was meant for ye, Baodan. Now, go and get her before she does something foolish."

* * *

He found her on the beach, staring into the ocean with enough sadness in her eyes to break his heart. Her hair blew around her face so wildly he knew she couldn't see him. He paused to watch her before approaching.

He watched as she glanced down at a small object she held in the palm of her hand. He couldn't make out what it was, but as she lifted her head and reared her arm back, he knew what she meant to do. His heart stopped.

He ran as fast as he could, diving into the water after the small rock she sent sailing into the air.

Chapter 21

For the life of me, I couldn't figure out what the hell he was doing. He floundered around in the water like a crazy man, and the shock of watching him do so made me stop crying.

I looked down at the pile of pebbles I held in my hand and realized. He thought I'd thrown Morna's rock. My heart started beating rapidly, and it frightened me just how quickly my mood shifted. I went from heartache to hope in the flick of an eye. I hadn't been wrong after all.

I shouted after him, but the waves were coming in so strong that he couldn't hear me. Reluctantly, I slipped off my leather footings and started to step into the water. I would get his attention no other way. There was no point in hiking up my dress, I would get soaked through anyway. Instead I just walked straight in, grabbing onto his arm as I reached him.

"Baodan." He didn't seem to feel me, his arms swinging wildy, his eyes wet. "Baodan, stop. What are you doing?" I knew, but wanted him to say.

When he finally registered that I stood next to him, he latched onto me, crushing me against him as he wrapped his arms around me. "Ach, Mitsy. How are ye here, lass?"

"What do you mean? Why wouldn't I be here?"

"The rock. I saw ye throw it, and ye just told me that ye were leaving." He carefully kissed the top of my head and stroked my hair, now frizzy and damp from the spray of the ocean.

"No, you didn't. I didn't throw Morna's rock. I just

chunked a bunch of pebbles into the ocean."

"What?" He leaned back and grabbed both sides of my face, turning my head upward so that I looked straight at him.

"You heard me. I didn't throw it, but what do you care anyhow? You didn't seem to mind that I planned to leave."

He kissed me then. A soft and short touch, but my heart danced in response to it.

"Ach, lass, I did care. 'Twas for that reason that I found meself too frightened to tell ye. I have been a fool."

I shivered uncontrollably. The water was freezing, and the windy night made it even cooler. "Can we get out of the water? Then you can tell me what a complete and total moron you've been."

I don't think the chill of the water bothered him at all. He looked surprised when I said it and then noticed my trembling arms. Before I could protest, he bent down and lifted me, carrying me like a babe out of the roaring ocean.

Once on shore, he carried me up to a nook in the high towering rocks that blocked the wind quite well. We didn't have anything dry, but he rubbed his hands up and down my arms to warm me and pulled me close to him once again.

I wouldn't be warm until I got into some dry clothes, but I wanted to finish our conversation before going back inside the castle. "Ok, you can continue now. You were telling me what a fool you are."

He chuckled and I delighted at the rise and fall of his chest as he did so. He was so sturdy, so beautiful.

"Aye, I was. I canna tell ye how sorry I am, lass. I know that I doona know ye well, but I doona believe I've ever cared for someone the way I do ye. 'Tis a different feeling, an unusual one, and I doona know what to do with it."

141

He was right. It was different, the feeling that spanned between us whenever we were near one another. "What do you mean you don't know what to do? You don't do anything, just let it come naturally."

"Aye, I wish it came so easily for me. I still doona know if I am capable of allowing someone into me life, but I would like to try. Please, doona leave."

I was so thrilled at his openness, I beamed all over. I knew what a step it was for him. "I'm not going to leave. Not yet, anyway. I never planned on it. I heard you outside Bri's door and I said it to get a reaction. When you gave me none, I became so angry I could have spit fire."

He surprised me by pinching me hard on the rear. A step for him as well. "'Twas a dirty trick. It broke me own heart to hear ye say that ye wished to leave with no a thought of me."

"Will we stay here a while?" I knew he wouldn't feel like he could.

"I canna do so. There are things at home that need me attention. Will ye come with me and stay at the castle? I know 'tis verra much of me to ask ye to return to the castle while Niall is there, but ye will be safe as long as I'm with ye. He willna be allowed in the castle any longer after I arrive." He shifted nervously. "'Tis no verra customary, but I doona care, and ye doona seem to me as the sort of lass who would mind it."

I would have loved to stay with Bri longer but she would understand. I couldn't pass up the chance of seeing where this led. "Yes, I'll come, and you're right. I don't give two squats about what's customary."

Chapter 22

The goodbyes were hard but not nearly as difficult as they would have been if I'd been going back to my own time to return to Texas. At least now, I knew I would see Bri and Adelle again. Even if I did eventually decide to leave here, I would make sure to see them before I left.

Baodan decided that we should stop at Cameron Castle to check in on his mother on our way back to McMillan Castle. I tried to gently persuade him otherwise, but he'd not relented. I didn't blame him, of course. Naturally, he worried after she'd been so ill very recently.

Still, it didn't make the thought of meeting her any more appealing. He could sense my nervousness and leaned forward to nibble at the base of my neck, but ended up with a mouthful of hair.

"Ye have lovely hair, lass, but how do ye have so much of it? I doona even think Artair here has as much as ye do. Did yer parents have locks such as that?"

How little we truly knew about one another. He didn't know anything about who I'd been before I came here, not that I'd been orphaned, or that I'd been married. Yet, I couldn't shake the feeling that it just wasn't very important. Those were all things he could learn in time and, while they played a part in making me who I was, he didn't need to know them to see the person I was now.

He could see what lay inside me without knowing

anything and, as long as he accepted that, I supposed it didn't matter how long we'd known one another. After all, I'd known Brian for years, and I would bet money that he wouldn't be able to tell anyone my favorite color, movie, or even birthday. Time meant little if the person you spent it with was a total numb nut.

"No." I leaned into him, relaxing my head against his chest. "Well, I actually don't know. I never knew either of my parents."

"Ach, lass, I'm verra sorry. What happened to them?"

"I don't know. They may still be alive actually, but part of me likes to hope not. I know that sounds horrible, but if they died, it means they didn't want to give me up."

He reached up to brush my hair so that it draped over one shoulder as he rested his chin on the other, his face pressed gently against mine. "Give ye up?"

"Yeah, it happens sometimes, if the parents feel they can't care for the child. I was bounced around from home to home until I was fourteen."

He dragged his hands up and down my thigh, rubbing them in comfort. "And what happened to ye then?"

"I was placed in the home of an old woman named Lilly, the only home that ever stuck. She was the closest thing I ever had to a mom, and I loved her very much. She passed away a few years ago, right after I graduated college."

"Ye know we took in Eoghanan much the same way ye speak of. All suspect it, but few know the truth of it. 'Tis no always blood that makes someone kin, aye?"

"Yes." It pleased me to hear him say such a thing about Eoghanan. Perhaps his guilt of assumption as to who assaulted me would soften him toward E-o and help him realize that no fault lay with Eoghanan.

He squeezed me tight and let out a soft sigh of sympathy, but I could tell he wanted to ask something.

"What?" I turned my head to kiss his cheek, and he grinned against my lips.

"What is college?"

I looked up to see several riders coming toward us. I tapped his knee to get his attention. "I'll tell you later, looks like we have visitors."

He smiled again as he spurred the horse on. "Indeed we do, lass. It seems that we are to cross paths with me mother."

* * *

She travelled in a small group. Two men, one of them Baodan's cousin, the laird of McMillan Castle, Griogair Cameron. The other a trusted friend called Henson.

As soon as we reached them and hellos were said all around, everyone dismounted. His mother surprised me by bypassing Baodan and coming straight over to me to greet me properly.

"I'm Kenna. Ye must be, Mitsy. I was right about ye, aye? Ye fell prey to one of Morna's spells?"

"Um...yes and, yes I did." Baodan glanced over at me before whisking the two men a little farther away. I supposed he didn't want to have to explain what his mother meant.

"And ye did find yer friend, aye? Did ye no wish to remain with the Conalls?"

I warmed suddenly. What should I say to her? *Yes, I did find her, but now I'm going to live with your son a while. Just so we can, ya know, see where it goes.* I did not want to be the one to explain anything to her, that was Baodan's job. "I did see them, yes, but Bri is very busy with her baby and I didn't want to intrude."

"Ah, so ye thought ye would play upon me son's sympathies and rely on his charity, aye?"

I didn't want to get off on the wrong foot with his mother, but her assumption seemed uncalled for, and I wasn't one to stifle what I thought just to make a good impression. "Excuse me? That's not what this is at all. Perhaps, you should talk to your son about it."

She smiled and laughed softly before moving to lace her arm with mine. "I like ye, lass, and so does Baodan. Just look at the way he keeps glancing over here at ye. I haven't seen him look that way in a verra long time. I only spoke in jest. I'm pleased to know that ye are no a lass to be ruled over."

I laughed shakily and smiled down at her, now much more at ease. "Where are you going? We were headed to Cameron Castle to see you."

"I am headed in the direction ye came from, toward Conall Castle. I have yet to see me niece and am anxious to love on the sweet babe."

I grinned thinking of the fat-cheeked, blue-eyed baby girl. "Well, she's sure a cutie."

"Aye, I'm sure she is. Let's go meet up with the lads so that each of us can be on our way. Griogair will be headed back to Cameron Castle now. He only means to escort me to the edge of his territory. Henson shall accompany me the rest of the way. I'd like us to make it much further before nightfall."

* * *

"Was she as frightening as ye imagined, lass?" He

whispered as we watched his mom and Henson ride in the direction of Conall Castle.

"No. She's great. Much like you. Although, it's hard to believe she fell as sick as you said. She seemed totally fine."

We re-mounted Artair and set out on our way before he spoke. "Aye, if I had no watched her wither away in her own bed for so many moons, I wouldna be able to believe it meself. I'm verra glad to see her doing so well, but something told to me before, haunts me now."

Worry and confusion echoed in his voice. I twisted around to look at him. "What do you mean?"

"'Twas Eoghanan who convinced her to leave when she was ill. I dinna understand why he would wish it. When I spoke to him about it, he told me to wait and see how much better she would feel once she was away from the castle. He was verra right."

"How could he have known that?"

He shrugged behind me. "I doona know, but 'tis certain I intend to find out as soon as we arrive."

I allowed the evening to pass by silently. Each time I glanced back at him, I could tell that his thoughts were very far away.

Chapter 23

As we approached McMillan Castle, I saw nothing of either brother. I couldn't have been more relieved. The closer we got to Baodan's home, the more I sensed that Baodan readied himself to pounce on Niall for what he had done to me. I didn't want to be anywhere around when he found him.

The entire situation with his mother also did nothing to help his mood. I had my own suspicions as to why Eoghanan believed his mother would be safer elsewhere, but while Baodan stewed, it was not the time for me to express them.

Eoghanan had been right to try and protect me from Niall and, after the little time I'd spent with the creep, I would put nothing past him. I couldn't imagine what would make any man, even one as disgusting as Niall, want to poison his own mother, but if someone inside the castle meant Kenna harm, my bet was on him.

The stables were empty as well, and I couldn't bear the stress in Baodan's face as he put Artair away in the stall. I walked around the horse and put my arms around him, reaching my hands up to kiss him thoroughly. Baodan's mood needed a lift.

It seemed to help a little. When we were both breathless, he grinned down at me, his previous worries gone if only for a second. "What was that for, lass?"

"Does it matter?"

"No. Are ye ready to go inside? I'll see ye settled so that ye may rest while I find me brother."

I sighed, disappointed. I hoped to distract him for a little longer, but clearly he would find no peace until he had dealt with Niall. "Yes, I'm ready."

He grabbed my hand and walked quickly. It pleased me to know that he thought enough not to bring me to the same room he'd placed me in before. He seemed to read my thoughts and looked sideways at me as we continued down a long hallway in the opposite wing from where I'd stayed before. "I will no ask ye to stay in the room ye were in before. I shall place ye in me own room, and I shall find rest elsewhere."

I looked up at him and frowned but said nothing. Why would he plan on sleeping somewhere else? I certainly didn't want him to.

He opened the door but didn't step inside. He merely motioned for me to enter. "Go ahead, lass. I shall have a warm bath brought up for ye and a clean dress. I shall join ye later, for I doona want ye to be in me home with me brother about. I willna be able to breathe freely with ye here until I see Niall gone from me home forever."

He started to leave but I stopped him. I knew he'd be angry with Eoghanan as well, and E-o didn't deserve to be punished for what Niall tried to do. "Hey, it's not Eoghanan's fault so don't try to make it his. He spent every moment outside my door until that last night. He truly didn't want to leave me, but something urgent required his attention. He worried about me. Promise me you won't punish him for this."

"Aye, I shall try no to do so, lass." He kissed me softly and left.

* * *

True to his word, a group of women arrived carrying steaming buckets of water so that I could have a relaxing bath.

I did not find it relaxing. Though nice to get clean, I felt as if I harbored woodland creatures in my hair, I worried endlessly while I sat in the large tub.

Not about Niall. If he still lingered around and tried to come near me, I'd take to his balls again and rip them right off this time. I did, however, worry about Baodan. He held on to too much anger and resentment, and I expected that he had done so for a good many years. I couldn't imagine what such bitterness would feel like living inside of you for so long. I had plenty of things to be angry about, but I always wound up utterly exhausted after getting all riled up for all of five minutes. It would be an exhausting life, staying angry all of the time.

Perhaps ridding himself of Niall would help some, but I doubted it. While I still couldn't see why, it wasn't Niall that he despised the most. What happened with me might have evened the playing field a little, but Baodan punished Eoghanan, not Niall, with every thought.

There had to be more to the story about what happened with his late wife than Eoghanan simply being unable to save her from a sickness. At least, I hoped so. If Baodan really did put so much blame on his brother for something like that, perhaps he wasn't really the man I considered him.

With the water growing colder with each passing second, I glanced around the room for something to dry myself. Seeing nothing, I frowned, stood, and did my best to shake off the water from the top half of my body. After wringing out my hair, I dressed in the clean gown and moved next to the fire to allow my hair to dry.

Five minutes later, impatience got the best of me, and I decided enough time had passed. How long did it take to tell someone to leave anyway? He'd be angry if he caught me outside of the room, but he would have to realize that he was not my keeper. I would not be ordered around without good reason, and I could see no reason for me to stay inside his room.

Besides, I wanted to explore the castle, right-side up and not in the hurried fashion I'd seen it in while escaping from Niall.

I moved quietly, pausing with nearly every footstep to listen for any sign of Baodan approaching. I hoped I could hear him coming and would be able to run back to his bedchamber before he got there.

I got only ten steps away from the bedchamber when a hand at my elbow caused me to stop.

"Ach, what are ye doing back here, lass?"

Rhona spun me around to face her. An odd combination of relief and confusion etched her face.

"What do you mean? Baodan brought me."

"Oh, the Laird is back? I am no so pleased to hear it. I canna stand to imagine what he thinks of me now."

I regarded her skeptically. "Did you not know? Who ordered a bath to be readied for me?"

She shook her head. "Baodan must have sent some of the girls up here himself, for I have been in the gardens, and to the gardens I shall return."

"Why? I'm sure Baodan would wish to see you."

"No, I doona believe that he would. I failed him and allowed something wretched to happen to ye. I canna apologize enough for it, lass."

She looked devastated, and I reached out a hand to comfort her. "You didn't allow anything. The fault is not

151

yours, and I don't think Baodan sees it that way either. Besides, nothing really happened to me."

"Oh, I'm glad that he dinna hurt ye, but it doesna release me of me failure."

Why did so many of these people feel a need to punish themselves for everything? I probably leaned too far in the other direction. I knew how likely I was to mess up pretty much anything, so I learned from a young age to forgive myself everything. "Yes, it does so."

"I willna argue with ye, lass, but ye simply doona understand. Baodan is no a forgiving man to those who fail him. I have cared for this family since he was a babe, but I doona doubt that he will wish me gone for no watching over ye while he was away. I am off to the village to gather a few things and pay a visit to me brother. I will be back in a few days and, by then, perhaps I will have the courage to face him."

"Um…okay. Well, have a safe trip." I stared at her wide-eyed as I watched her walk away. She seemed almost frightened of Baodan, and it made me uneasy.

My first impressions of him, after realizing he wasn't the role-playing weirdo that I assumed at first, was that he seemed kind, generous, and just a little broken. Broken was okay, but secretive and mean wasn't.

His seemingly unreasonable ill-feelings toward his brother, and Rhona's fear of him now, had me second-guessing my decision to come here. To press him about the truth might push him away further, but it had to be done.

I needed to know what he hid from me.

Chapter 24

He knew how hard Durell worked for him, but creating the antidote moved slowly. With each day, Eoghanan grew more concerned that Niall would harm another before he could find him.

Three days passed with no sign of Niall in the village. He looked for him the first night but, after finding him nowhere, Eoghanan decided his time would be better spent aiding in the creation of the antidote. He spent nearly every moment at Durell's side assisting him in whatever way he could, and today Durell tasked him with gathering more herbs.

On his way to do just that, Eoghanan saw three young lassies huddled together whispering. They caught his eye immediately, and it only took him a moment to realize why. Two of the girls, the youngest ones, were Niall's conquests, young girls who'd been tricked into bed and then quickly removed from it.

The third lass and by far the oldest, was Greta, the only woman Eoghanan had ever seen enter his brother's bedchamber twice. While she didn't receive money for the services she offered men, he knew the married woman to be a bedtime favorite for many lads in the village.

He could see the women out of the corner of his eye as they watched him, smiling as they paused to laugh between hushed words. They had no reason to be talking about him. He socialized with no one, and he'd not joined any of them in bed.

Perhaps they spoke of his brother and watched him to ensure that he couldn't hear.

Staring them down so that they would prepare for his approach, Eoghanan moved toward them. "Morning, lassies. Do any of ye happen to know where I could find Niall?"

The younger girls said nothing, only stared at him with wide eyes in terror at being found out. Intimidated by no one, Greta allowed her eyes to roam up and down him. "Why would any of us know? As ye can see, he is no with us now."

Eoghanan moved closer so that they stood around each other in a tight circle. He couldn't be easily intimidated either. "Aye, I can see that just fine. Is yer husband away again?" Greta's face showed nothing, and Eoghanan knew that he assumed correctly. "Aye, I dinna think that he would be. He stays away often does he no? If I followed ye home, would I find Niall in yer bed? Let us go and see, shall we?"

He started to move away from them but stopped as Greta ran to block his path. "No, ye willna find him in me bed. While I'll no deny that I did see him two days ago, he couldna join anyone in bed."

"What do ye mean by that, Greta?" He remembered Rhona's mention of his limp. He must have been injured badly. The thought brought Eoghanan great joy.

"'Twas just what I told these lassies about. He told me quite willingly, though I canna imagine why he would have wanted anyone to know."

"Well, what was it?" He needed to know so that he could get the herbs back to Durell. If Niall had truly been gone for two days, he had little time to get the antidote. Niall could reach nearly anywhere he wished within a few more days.

"I'm telling ye, am I no?" Greta stared at him briefly,

rolling her eyes before she continued. "He said that ye had a whore staying at the castle, which surprised me. I would think our Laird wouldna need to pay for the company of a lass, but 'tis no matter. He tried to purchase her. The lass refused but eventually gave into him, but it was no for long. After she had him naked, she apparently injured his," she paused and glanced down at herself. "He said it hurt him so badly he couldna stop her before she fled the castle."

Eoghanan let out a large breath of relief. At least, Mitsy got away from him. The lass was fiery and smart. No doubt she would have found her way to the Conalls by now. "So he came to ye for what reason?"

"I doona know. He couldna do what he usually wants to when he pays me a visit. He simply rested for a day and then went on his way."

"Did he say where he was going?" He feared he already knew the answer.

"He said that he was traveling to Cameron Castle. That he wished to see yer mother."

Eoghanan said nothing as he turned and left them, running as fast as he could back to Durell's. He knew getting their mother away from McMillan Castle to be only a temporary solution. For that reason, he hoped to have proof of all Niall had done before Baodan returned. Once Baodan returned to McMillan Castle, Eoghanan knew Niall would leave to go after their mother again.

Rushing inside the old man's small home, he threw the herbs in the alchemist's direction. "How much longer, Durell? I need the antidote immediately."

The old man shook his head, and Eoghanan's heart sank.

"I am close, sir, but it willna be ready for at least another day."

Eoghanan slumped against the wall as grief took him. It would be too late by then. He couldn't reach his mother in time, nor could he send her warning. She would be dead before the antidote was ever prepared.

* * *

McMillan Castle

His brothers were not anywhere on the castle grounds. Niall, must have fled after realizing the magnitude of his mistake. Baodan could only hope that he would have the sense to never return.

Eoghanan, he suspected could be found in the village, for wouldn't run from his mistakes, even the ones not truly his. Mitsy was right. What Niall tried to do to her was no more Eoghanan's fault than what happened to Osla. Why had it taken him so many years to see?

Anger filled him, anger at Niall, and anger at himself for what he'd become. Too many years of regrets and frustrations built up inside him, and he could take it no longer.

Years of expecting more from himself than those around him and years of believing that unhappiness formed protection had protected him from nothing. In the end, they'd only kept him from truly living at all.

He would choose to live now. Damn anyone who tried to stop him from doing so. He hoped that confronting Niall would release some of his frustration. Now unable to do so, he only hoped the lass in his bedchamber could take what came for her.

He was a man in need, more now than ever before in his

life. He denied himself of her once out of a foolish sense of honor. He would not do so again. Tonight he would explore every bit of her, lay claim to all that she had to give him and let go of all his frustrations.

Freedom lay inside her, and he would bury himself deep within to find it.

Chapter 25

I intended to speak with him as soon as he returned from sending Niall away, to demand that he tell me what really happened between him and Eoghanan. All of my well-laid intentions flew out the door the moment he walked back into the bedchamber.

He looked hungry, needy, and not for food. There'd been a similar look in his eyes as we lay next to each other the night we made camp next to Alec, but it had been restrained, muffled. He didn't gauge his expression now, and the intensity of his gaze frightened me.

"Are you ok? What did you say to him?"

He didn't move from inside the doorway, only reached behind him to latch the door. Baodan tensed and seemed to tower over everything inside the room, even more so than he usually did.

He rolled his neck from side to side, and I found myself unconsciously backing up until my back hit the wall behind me.

"Hello?" My word sounded small and, by the looks of him, I knew he hadn't heard me. I couldn't tell if he was angry or horny, but I swallowed as he moved toward me. Every inch of my body seemed to sense his approach.

He didn't stop moving until he stood close enough to brace both of his hands against the wall, leaving me trapped between his arms. Finally, he spoke. "Niall is no here, neither is Eoghanan."

"Oh, okay." I ducked underneath his arms and scooted

down the wall, but I barely stepped away from him before he moved, blocking my path, leaving me trapped once more.

"Where do ye think ye are going, lass?" He leaned forward, his voice deep and slow as he spoke with his face pressed against mine. The words reverberated down my spine as my whole body trembled at the sensation.

"Um...nowhere. I'm just moving across the room. So, did you decide where you're going to sleep?" Not that I wanted him to sleep elsewhere, I wasn't afraid of him, but the intensity of his gaze and movements intimidated me. I could tell where this was leading. Although not inexperienced, with the mood he seemed to be in, I didn't know if I had the energy to keep up.

He laughed as he leaned forward and gave a light bite to my earlobe, talking in between the kisses that he trailed down the side of my neck and over my collarbone. Goose bumps spread all over my body.

"I changed me mind. I doona intend to sleep elsewhere, lass. No if ye doona mind me staying here with ye."

He didn't ask it as a question, and he gave me no chance to respond before he moved his kisses lower, touching his lips along the lining of my cleavage. My chest rose and fell, meeting his lips each time he went to touch a different part of my breasts uncovered by the gown.

"Ye doona mind, do ye?" His words were almost a growl as he moved up the other side of my neck and proceeded to nibble on my ear lobe.

"No, I wouldn't say I mind. What's gotten into you?" I asked the question breathlessly, but I had to know the answer. I wasn't sure he'd ever loosen up enough to ever actually do anything besides kiss me, but I certainly never expected him to change his tune so suddenly. He moved confidently, unburdened by whatever held him back before. It pleased me to no end. Bossy Baodan was so sexy I wouldn't have been surprised if my entire gown just melted off my body. My skin burned.

He moved to my lips and kissed me ravenously before answering my question. As he pulled away, he kept one hand at the lowest part of my back, pressing me against him. The other slid up to my shoulder, pulling my dress down until the upper part of my arm was showing. "Ye, lass, 'twas no only the witch that sent ye here who possesses magic, for I know ye do as well. I have spent much of the past years acting as a fool. None have been able to make me see that until ye. Now," he paused for just a moment and grinned down at me, "lift up yer arms."

I did, first pulling my other arm out of the sleeve before lifting them up slowly, enjoying the look of torturous delight on his face. Once they were up, he all but charged me, crushing his mouth so hard to mine that I tasted blood. His kiss would bruise me, but I could not have cared less.

He moved his hands to the top of my dress and pulled so hard that stitches popped as it fell below my breasts. I gasped as my nipples brushed against his chest. When his hands cupped them, he groaned deep into my mouth.

I nibbled his lower lip and reached up to stop the kiss, to pull his head down to my breasts. He didn't fight me, and his eyes widened as he actually saw my breasts for the first time. He groaned as he sucked the peaked bud deeply into his mouth, and my stomach grew taut at the sensation. My knees grew weak as he flicked my nipples with his tongue, the painful tugs exquisitely delightful.

The wall was all that held me up as his lips reclaimed my mouth and his hand reached underneath my dress. I could not keep steady. After my bath, there'd been nothing in the way of underwear, so I was bare beneath the gown. As he caressed my center, I moaned as my knees nearly gave way.

He held me tight against him, not allowing me to fall as he explored me intimately. His hips moved against me. My dress barely hung on, and I reached down to feel him underneath his kilt as his hardness rocked against my dress. He groaned loudly as I grabbed him, and his lower lip trembled from the touch.

I'd known his largeness from feeling his length against me the night in the woods, but holding his erection in my hands made me tremble in anticipation.

"You can't leave yourself like this, again. I'm not going to let you. "

He knew what I referred to, and I released him as he pulled away from me. Grinning, he shed his kilt. I stared at him googly-eyed until he moved toward me. He bent and scooped me up as he carried me to the bed, working the laces on the back of my gown as he did so.

"I'm pleased to hear it, lass, for I will no deny meself the pleasure of claiming ye a moment more."

Chapter 26

It took only one yank for the dress to loosen enough for him to pull it away from her. As he slipped it from the rest of her body and looked down at her, he felt his heart might stop. Baodan lay her on the bed and stepped away so that he could look upon her. She was more beautiful than he'd imagined. The vibrant red hair against the paleness of her skin, the smooth lines, and full breasts were enough to make him throb with the need to get inside her.

She looked up at him with anticipation and a sense of trust so complete that it broke his heart. He could not do what he wanted to most in the world. He could not lay claim to her as he wished, as he promised himself and told her he would only moments ago.

He needed her too much, his desire too strong. If he let himself enter her, he would lose himself in it, in the sensation of being inside a woman. All else would fade away, and the act would become more about forgetting his shame for the resentment he allowed himself to hold onto, than the love he knew he felt for her.

If it had been another woman he found in his bed, he would use her in the way he needed. No matter the pain it caused him, he could not bring himself to do so to Mitsy. She could pull him from darkness, and she deserved more than to be the vessel with which he emptied his frustrations.

She deserved his love and honesty. His love, she had, although he could not bring himself to tell her just yet. She warmed his cold heart the first moment he saw her, and she captured it completely the first time she fell asleep against his chest the night he saw her running into the woods.

He suspected she felt much the same way, but it wouldn't be fair of him to allow her to love him when he'd been dishonest with her. He could not sleep with her and claim more of her heart before she knew the truth about his wife's tragic demise. For if it caused her to feel differently, she deserved the chance to get away before he lay claim to the most precious part of a woman.

"What are you doing?"

She crawled toward him, wrapping her arms around his neck, keeping her knees on the bed, her breasts pressed flush against him. Enough temptation to pull him from his thoughts.

He kissed her gently, and she tensed in his arms. She was no fool, and he knew she sensed the change in him before he uttered a word.

"Nope. You're not doing this again. I'm not letting you beat yourself up over something like sex. You're allowed to have it. People have it all the time, and me and you," she paused and pointed her finger to each of them. "are having it tonight. So get that terrible look off your face and strap in because this is totally about to go down."

He wrapped his arms around her and laughed into her hair. She said the strangest things, and he loved all of them. Lifting her hair, he gently kissed her neck as he reached for a covering to drape over her. She frowned at him, clearly annoyed as he did so.

"I'm sorry, lass, but I canna do so tonight."

Her face changed and he watched as she pulled the blanket more tightly around her, realizing she didn't understand him.

"Why?"

She thought that he didn't want her.

He pulled her into his arms and kissed her until she melted against him once more. Crawling onto the bed with her, he motioned for her to follow him. Once they lay next to one another, he reached up to cradle her face in his hands. "There is no anything that I want more than to live inside ye this night."

"Then, do it."

He smiled but shook his head as he continued. "I canna, lass. Ye deserve more than what I can give ye this moment. 'Tis been far too long since I have been with a woman. If I lay with ye now, 'twould be more about satisfying that need than what it should. I care about ye too much to do that."

She rolled her eyes at him and he snuggled closer. "There is also something that I must tell ye. For once ye know it, ye may feel differently than ye do now. I willna lay claim of ye until ye know what it is."

"Fine. What is it?"

She spoke short, and he couldn't deny that it pleased him to know how disappointed she seemed not to have him.

"'Tis about me wife that died. Osla dinna pass the way I said."

Her face softened as she reached out to grab his hand. He couldn't help but feel that perhaps she suspected his lie.

"We were happy for a while. I was at least. I loved her verra much, but something wasna right inside her after we married. She dinna smile or talk often. She wouldna hardly leave the bed and spoke often of her hatred for living."

He paused to gauge her reaction, but she gave nothing of her thoughts away. Her gaze remained sure and steady, and he did his best to continue.

"I went away for a short time and left Eoghanan to watch over her. She was in the darkest place I'd ever seen her. I worried every moment while away. I returned to find her dead. She'd hung herself out one of the windows. I blamed Eoghanan for too long, but he isna the one who deserves the blame for what happened to her."

Baodan swallowed the lump that built in his throat at the mention of Osla and closed his eyes to distance himself from the moment. Mitsy's hand moved to his face, and he opened his eyes to see her staring at him in astonishment.

"And you think the person who is to blame is really you?"

He nodded, the shame rising within him once again. "Aye, I wasna able to save her. I couldna be enough for her, and the knowledge of that drove her to end her life."

Mitsy surprised him by leaning forward to kiss him. She held her lips there, unmoving, and he sighed as some of the tension within him fled.

"I don't know what it is with you that makes you punish yourself so completely. You're right to say that Eoghanan is not to blame, but neither are you."

"How can ye say that, lass? 'Twas me job to protect her, and I failed. I dinna make her happy, and she couldna bear it."

Mitsy shook her head at him, "It was not your job to make her happy. That is something one must do on her own, and you are not to blame for the sickness in her mind. It is horrible when someone has such sadness inside them, but you are not the cause of her pain."

He said nothing. Perhaps she spoke true. He did nothing but treat Osla with respect and love. Why, when Mitsy suggested something to him, it made perfect sense, but he could not reach the same conclusions on his own?

"Is that why you hesitated? You were afraid that I would blame you as well and wouldn't want you? That I'd worry that you wouldn't be enough for me?"

He could scarcely look at her as he answered. He feared nothing more. He'd not cared for anyone in the way he cared for Mitsy. He couldn't bear the thought of her leaving when things had only just begun between them. "Aye."

"You are a silly fool. I'd not given it much thought until now, but seeing as you're so harsh on yourself, I wonder if you're so harsh on others. There's something I haven't told you yet, either. Perhaps when you hear it, you won't find me so appealing."

He looked up at her and shook his head at the ridiculousness of her suggestion. The only person he'd ever judged as harshly as himself was Eoghanan, and he would make amends for that soon. She could say nothing to make him love her less. "No, I'm afraid that ye are stuck with me affections, whether ye wish them or no. Ye are faultless in me eyes, no matter what it is that ye have to say."

"Still, I will have it said. Then you can never use this excuse not to be with me ever again. The next time you get me all riled up like that and don't do anything to release the pressure, I'll give you the same treatment I gave your lousy brother. Understand?"

He laughed deeply. "Aye, I am too attached to all of me parts to allow ye to do that, lass. Get on with whatever ye must say."

"I was married once, too."

His eyes widened and she stared at him. He'd not considered the possibility but, now that she said it, he didn't know why. He knew her to be younger than him but older than most of the lasses around here were when they married. Of course she would have a past from her own time. "Ach, I'm sorry, lass. How did he die?"

"He didn't. Unfortunately, he's alive and well, and banging some girl while living in my old house."

Though not a word he knew, he understood what 'banging' meant well enough, it was what she said about him still being alive that had him nervous. "If he dinna die, does that mean that ye are still married to him?"

"No. I'll admit that I'm no history buff, but I'm pretty certain even if it's allowed, it's not very common around here yet. We're divorced, which means that we are no longer married. Thank God. I'm pretty certain he was sleeping with at least one other person the entire time we were together. Scum bag."

The idea of someone treating her so poorly angered him. How could any man wish to be with another when he had her? "I'm verra sorry, lass. If he wasna four hundred years ahead of me, I would verra much like to harm him for the pain he caused ye. But I dinna lie to ye before. It does nothing but make me admire ye all the more. Ye have been through much, and ye have no let it harden ye as I have done."

He inhaled as she pressed herself flat against him, and he moaned as she slipped her hand in between him, latching onto his length. "What do ye think ye are doing, lass? I told ye, I willna have ye tonight. I wish to do so when I can worship ye no blind with need."

"You're not as hardened as you seem to think. Well, with the exception of this part. " She ran her hand up and down him as his entire body trembled at the sensation. "You don't have

167

to have me tonight, but it seems you're forgetting what I told you. I'm not going to let you go to bed in this state. It's not healthy."

He loved the lass, just lying next to her made him feel as if he could be the person he'd not allowed himself to be since Osla's passing. He wished to tell her, but as she slid herself down him and wrapped her mouth around the most intimate part of him, he found himself incapable of speech.

It was not the time anyhow. If he said the words now, while she drew such indescribable pleasure from him, the words would not seem sincere, and he wished them to mean something to her for they certainly did to him.

Tomorrow, he would have to love every bit of her tenfold to make up for the pleasure she gifted him. Closing his eyes, he lost himself as Mitsy explored him in a way no lass had ever done before.

Chapter 27

"Doona ye move, lass. Stay in bed. I shall find us something to eat."

Still very sleepy, I tried to sit up to smile at him as he started to leave. My hair must have looked a mess for he grinned as I did. I glanced up to find my hair sticking out so wildly I could see it in my peripherals. "Yeah, I know, I'm a messy sleeper, and I look ridiculous when I wake up. Always."

"Ye look beautiful, lass. I'll be back."

Once he left, I stretched myself out over the bed as I smiled at the ceiling. I'd been wrong to question the sort of man he was, and it relieved me that he chose to tell me the truth without me having to guilt it out of him.

I looked over to the window and, judging by the height of the sun, guessed it to be somewhere around midday. I expected it was highly unusual for Baodan to stay in bed so long but, after what I'd done for him, he seemed one happy camper.

He spent the rest of the night holding me, whispering in between kisses how he planned to repay my kindness. I tried to talk him into just doing it then, but he was nothing if not stubborn. If he said it wasn't going to happen that night, it wasn't going to happen.

Reluctantly, I let my frustration go and passed the rest of the night just content to be in his arms. Our confessions changed something between us. A tangible sense of closeness not quite as strong before now bound us even more.

It seemed ridiculous to me that I would fall so quickly, but I could no longer deny that I had done just that. Baodan differed from anything I ever thought I wanted, but something about that made him seem even more right.

I'd never been around a man who spent as much time thinking as he did. He over-analyzed everything, always so worried about screwing up. It caused him constant grief, but it also made him considerate, thoughtful, and concerned. He was a true gentleman in every sense of the word – to the point of annoyance.

I could not have dreamed up someone more opposite from myself. He was quiet while I was loud, careful while I was rash, solemn while I was goofy. We seemed to view the world in very different ways, not that it should have been surprising since we came from very different worlds.

It seemed to me that I felt balanced in his presence, protected and content in a way I'd never felt with any man before. Although I knew it should've seemed foolish, there was such truth in the way I felt, I knew it couldn't be. I was in love with him.

Just as the thought crossed my mind, he re-entered the room carrying bread, cheese, and what appeared to be some sort of very strong smelling ale. Not my usual breakfast to be sure, but if brought to me in bed, I wouldn't complain.

"'Tis all I could find. It seems that Rhona disappeared along with both of me brothers, and I have told everyone else in the castle to enjoy a day in the village. We have the castle to ourselves."

"Oooh, how nice. I do know where Rhona is though."

He raised both eyebrows at me as he motioned for me to crawl out of the bed to eat. Why didn't it surprise me that he would be concerned with crumbies? "Ye do, lass? How do ye know that?"

"Well, don't get mad, but when you left me in here yesterday, I sort of snuck out after my bath. I bumped into Rhona about three steps outside of the door. She said she planned to see a family member for a few days. She seemed very worried you were going to be angry with her for what happened to me."

"Hmm...it seems that I have many apologies to make once she and Eoghanan choose to return. I can only see one reason why she would expect that of me. She has seen me poor treatment of Eoghanan all these years."

He looked down, and I reached out to squeeze his hand. "Hey. The past is not worth worrying over. If that's all everybody did, nobody would ever get anything done. You'll apologize to them later. Don't let it ruin the day."

He smiled and pulled me toward him to kiss me. "Ye are right, lass, as ye seem to be always. I have something planned for ye this evening."

"Will it involve clearing this debt between us that you spoke of last night?" I smiled against his cheek, and my pulse quickened at the thought of it.

"Aye, lass. I intend to re-pay ye in such a way that it is ye who is in debt."

* * *

Evening could not come fast enough, and I spent the day trying to push the sun out of the sky with my mind. I didn't succeed, but eventually night did come.

I watched the anticipation build within him throughout the day, and mine would've done the same had I not been ready to roll since the same time yesterday evening. I could also see that he seemed nervous, and I suspected I knew why.

He felt the same way I did. I saw the love in his eyes when he watched or even laughed at me, I heard it in his voice when he spoke, and I felt it in the soft stroke of his fingers as he held me close and played with my endless strands of hair.

I suspected that he wanted to tell me tonight, but I hoped to beat him to the punch. I wasn't entirely sure if he believed that I didn't blame him for what happened to his wife, and I wanted him to know that it did nothing to change what I thought of him.

As soon as he led me outside the castle, I knew where we went. To the pond, his favorite place. "What are we doing? Skinny dipping?"

He looked back at me, his eyebrows pinched together as they always did when I said something he thought strange. They stayed pinched a good deal of the time.

"What is that, lass?"

"Swimming, but without any clothes on."

"Is there another way to swim? I doona much like to get in the water with me clothes on."

I laughed as we reached the water's edge. "Well, in my time, most people wear tight suits when they go swimming, just to keep their private parts, ya know, private."

"That's what the water is for, lass. And the moon. It will keep yer parts from being seen." He smiled as he ripped off his kilt, not even remotely shy about standing naked in front of me. He glanced up at the dark sky and then frowned. "I doona think I thought of all this, lass. I like seeing yer private parts. Perhaps, we shouldna go for a swim."

"Nuh uh, you already planned it. We're going for a swim." I slipped out of my gown and jumped into the water before he could stop me. It froze me, and I breached the surface gasping and yelping as my entire body tightened up in response to the cold water.

Baodan laughed and dove in after me. Reaching for me, he pulled me tight against him as he ran his hands up and down my arms to warm me.

"This water is fricking freezing!"

"What did ye expect, lass? 'Tis summer, but ye do know where ye are, aye? 'Tis warm where ye are from?"

We swam in circles around each other and slowly I warmed. "It can get pretty cold in the winter, but most of the time, it's much warmer than this. The summers, oh gracious, they're hot."

He moved toward me and grabbed my hand, tugging me gently to an edge of the pond diagonally across from us. "Are ye any warmer?"

"Yes."

He stopped swimming. The pond seemed to shallow in this area because he stood as he dragged me across the water, only stopping once I floated in front of him. "Float backwards, lass."

I did and quickly bumped into a smooth ledge behind me. Placing my hands on top of it, I pushed myself up so that I sat on its edge. It set just deep enough beneath the water so that my breasts bobbed like apples on top of the surface, and its width allowed me to easily lean back into a wall of rock.

Once seated, Baodan stepped closer to me, grabbing each of my knees and spreading my legs so that he could step in between them. "I love the water, lass."

"I know you do. Do you know what I love?"

He grabbed my hands and pulled me close to him, so close that I could feel him hard against the lowest part of my stomach. "What's that, lass?"

"You." I blurted it out rather unromantically, but I never did well at that stuff so I'd not really expected it to sound eloquent. I just wanted him to know so that he could love me without the doubt of whether I returned his love.

"Ach, Mitsy." He rarely said my name, and he said nothing else as he grabbed the back of my head, leaning me backward so that he could kiss me while exploring me intimately beneath the water with his fingers.

I gasped into his mouth as he slipped two of his fingers inside me, the rush of water accompanied them only a glimpse of the fullness I knew would come soon. After ensuring that my center was warm and ready, he moved his caressing to the bud above it, creating an effortless friction as the water allowed his fingers to slide easily over the tender flesh.

Exquisite torture. As everything inside of me built, I slid against him, moaning as his lips explored every inch of my mouth, neck, and breasts. I neared release, but I didn't wish to climax without him. I wanted him to be a part of me as I did so, to feel him quiver as I clenched around him.

I reached up and grabbed his hair, tugging it roughly as I begged him. "I need you. Please, Baodan. Please."

"And I ye, lass."

He needed no more encouragement. He lifted me effortlessly so that he could adjust himself for entry. I took a deep breath as I waited. In the span of one heartbeat, he thrust inside me, filling me so completely that I felt I couldn't breathe without him.

As he moved inside me, nothing existed outside the rhythm we set with one another. I couldn't tell where we each began and ended. When release came, we shuttered in one another's arms, trembling as we slowly fell back to Earth.

Afterward, he moved to sit next to me on the ledge, kissing me and cleansing me with the water as I lay in the nook of his arm, resting against his chest.

He leaned forward to kiss the side of my head and whispered gently, his voice still shaky and breathless, "Will ye look at me, lass? I wish to tell ye something."

Weak and happy, I turned to see what he had to say, but the sound of rapidly approaching hooves interrupted us.

Baodan leapt out of the water to retrieve his kilt before the rider arrived. "Stay in the water so that ye are covered, lass."

Concern etched his face. I could tell by the way the rider approached that he carried terrible news. As the man started to slow his pace, Baodan called out to him. "What is it, man? What news do ye bring here so urgently?"

"'Tis yer cousin, Laird Cameron. He's dead."

Chapter 28

The details behind Griogair's death made little sense. Nor did the sudden disappearance of his mother. According to the messenger, they found Laird Cameron collapsed over a plate of food in his mother's empty cottage. With Nairne nowhere to be found.

Baodan stood for only a moment before he pushed aside his shock to make preparations. He directed his words to the rider. "I need ye to ride into the village for me. Gather up Rhona and all from the castle who I sent away from here today. Tell them to return at once for I must leave verra soon."

Everything but my head remained submerged beneath the water and, without him next to me, the water grew very cold once again.

"Aye, sir." The man started to turn his horse but paused and faced Baodan once more. "I forgot to tell ye, sir. Yer brother, Niall, has stepped in to watch over things until Lady Cameron is found and new arrangements can be made. He must have been only miles from the castle when Laird Cameron passed for he arrived at the castle only moments after they found his body. 'Twas fortunate timing."

My entire body shivered at the thought. There was nothing fortunate about it. While Baodan knew what a monster Niall could be, I doubted he suspected him of murder. I, on the other hand, could see it all too well. The timing of the incident just seemed too strange.

Baodan frowned and stepped closer to the messenger. "Why was he there, lad? Do ye know?"

"I believe he intended to pay a visit to yer mother, sir. But she had already moved on to Conall Castle by the time he arrived."

Thank God. I didn't like the idea of Kenna being there amongst the madness that now consumed Cameron Castle. She would be well-protected with the Conalls.

"Ah, I see. Thank ye, lad. Now ride as fast as ye can to the village for I need them to return quickly, aye?"

"Aye, sir."

With that, the man left. Baodan quickly grabbed my dress before moving to stand beside me so that I could climb out of the water to dress.

Once I completed my task, Baodan pulled me against him, wrapping his arms around me, not to warm me but to comfort himself.

"I'm so sorry." I whispered it against his chest, and he kissed the top of my head gently.

"As am I, lass. I canna make sense of it. I can think of none who would wish my cousin dead."

I shivered against Baodan. I didn't know what to say. With Nairne gone and Niall suddenly running the castle, I couldn't imagine what ran through his mind.

"Let's get ye inside, lass. I canna leave ye here alone, but I willna take ye to Griogair's burial. No with Niall there."

"What about his mother? Do you think...?" I couldn't finish.

Baodan reached for my hand as we proceeded to the castle. "I think that she is alive and well. She was either no there when Griogair died or she made her escape. I willna allow meself to believe otherwise until we know for certain. She deserves our hope, and I will give it to her. I am only glad that me own mother left before all of this occurred. 'Tis a relief to know that she is in safe hands."

"Yes, I'm glad, too." He walked quickly, and eventually I pulled away from his hand. It was easier for me to keep up with him that way. "What about Eoghanan?"

"I doona know where he is, but it doesna matter. I canna wait on him to arrive here, for I doona know when that will be."

"Will they…will they bury your cousin if his mother isn't there?"

We now stood inside his bedchamber, and he quickly started a fire, wrapping me in a blanket so I would warm. Despite all that happened, he still took the time to show me care. It didn't matter that he'd been unable to return my feelings with his words. I knew how he felt, and I knew that's what he'd been about to do when the messenger had arrived. There would be other days for sharing.

"Aye, lass, they willna wait to do so. As soon as Rhona arrives, I will leave. I need to be there for his sisters. I doona wish to let Niall near Griogair's wife and child."

My eyes widened at the thought of him creeping in on a widow. Niall wouldn't hesitate to do so. "Yeah, I don't blame you."

"Aye, he doesna need to get settled in his new position, for he willna be laird of Cameron Castle. Whether it be me own territory or no, I willna allow it."

"Ye willna allow what?" As if summoned, Rhona appeared in the doorway and Baodan rushed over to greet her.

"Niall to be laird of Cameron Castle. Laird Cameron is dead, and I must ride for there at once." He leaned forward and grabbed her hand so that he could kiss it. "I'm happy to see ye,

Rhona. I owe ye an apology, lass. I know 'twas no yer fault, I never believed it to be. But 'tis me own fault that I behaved in such a way that ye would expect me to be angry with ye."

Rhona's face softened dramatically, and she reached up to lay the back of her hand against his cheek. "I am sorry as well. I know who ye are inside, Baodan, and in me own distress I dinna trust it. Be gone with ye. I'll take good care of the lass while ye are away."

"Aye, I know that ye will." He moved over to stand next to me, grabbing both sides of my face as he kissed me gently. "Ye are the loveliest lass I have ever known. I shall think of the way ye feel in me arms every instant that I am away. I will return to ye soon. Make no mistake."

He left quickly and I stood at the window as I watched him ride away, not moving until he disappeared from my view.

* * *

The next morning, Rhona seemed friendlier than I'd ever seen her and moved busily about me in the castle kitchens trying to prepare whatever I wished.

"I'm fine, really." I'd already eaten enough food to last me a week and, truth was, if she tried to force anything else down my throat, I knew I might throw up. Standing to avoid another round of food, I moved to the doorway. "Can I ask you a question, Rhona?"

"O'course ye can, lass. What is it that ye need? I'm pleased that Baodan dinna wish for ye to be locked in the bedchamber this time."

"Oh geez, I am too. Listen, I can't stand to do nothing all day. It's not in my nature, and I'm worried anyhow. Lying around will kill me. Is there anything I can do around here to help you? Anything I can do to keep busy?"

She smiled wide and moved next to me, pointing up the staircase. "I'm pleased that ye are no satisfied to spend yer days abed. Far too many lassies find it pleasing, and 'tis how death finds ye. I doona plan to slow down long enough for it to ever catch me."

I laughed as I waited for her to give me some direction. "Good plan."

She grinned at herself and continued. "Lady Kenna is much the same way as yerself, lass. Before she fell ill, she busied herself by working in the room at the verra top of the castle. See," she pointed upstairs. "All the way to the top. I doona think she would mind if ye piddled in there. Looked through the books. Perhaps ye can figure out how she meant to place them and aid her in the quest to clean the room up a bit."

"Perfect." It sounded like tedious work, which was just what I needed. Something to require enough concentration so that I would not have enough time to worry. "I'll go there now."

She waved me on, and I smiled over my shoulder at her as I walked out of the kitchen. Directly into a very distressed Eoghanan.

Chapter 29

"E-o! Where have you been?" Dark circles lined his red eyes and his face seemed abnormally pale, making him appear visibly shaken. He looked as if he hadn't slept in days.

"Ach, lass."

He gripped me tightly as he pulled me against him in such a way that it seemed like I had known him for years.

"I am pleased to see that ye are well. I knew that ye would be, but I was still verra worried about ye. Where is Baodan? I must speak with him at once. We must leave for Cameron Castle immediately. I have reason to believe that our mother is in grave danger."

"Wait. What?" I pulled back so that I could look at him straight on. I assumed that his cousin's death upset him, but he spoke of something else. "Why are you worried about your mother? She's not at Cameron Castle." Shock immediately spread across his face, and I reached out to lay a reassuring hand on his arm. "You don't know what's happened, do you?"

"Oh God, I knew I would be too late. I was verra afraid that I would be, but I had hope. I hoped that…"

He stopped as he broke down into a sob. I put my arm around him as I moved him to sit down on one of the steps at the bottom of the staircase. "Hey, calm down. I think you're mistaken. You don't even know what's happened. Too late for what?"

"She's dead, is she no?"

I sat next to him and grabbed his hand, shaking it against his knee so that he would look up at me. "Your mother? No, she's not dead. I told you, she's not at the Camerons'. She's at Conall Castle. She went to see the new baby. It's your cousin, Griogair, who is dead."

"I'm sorry, lass, I doona understand."

He was such a mess. He needed a bath, a meal, and some sleep. Still, I knew that he would find none of those until he knew what happened. "They found Laird Cameron collapsed over the dining table in his mother's cottage, and they can't find Nairne anywhere. In the meantime, Niall stepped in until arrangements for a new Laird can be made."

Eoghanan's eyes darted back and forth as I watched his tired brain try to understand all that I'd said.

"God, lass. All of this wasna his plan, but he willna let it deter him for long. Ye said that me mother is no at Cameron Castle? I am pleased to hear it."

"Yes, she's at the Conalls'. Whose plan?" He looked away suddenly, and I knew he'd not meant to tell me all that he had.

"I should have said nothing to ye, lass. 'Tis no yer concern. 'Tis Baodan I need to speak to."

"Well, Baodan's not here and, unless you plan on riding after him, which you are in no shape to do, I think you should just tell me." I leaned back so that Rhona could see me inside the kitchen, and I waved to get her attention. "Will you get E-o something to eat? I swear he's about to fall over."

For a brief moment, Eoghanan's frown faded and he grinned at me weakly. "Thank ye, lass. I could indeed use a good meal, but I thought I told ye no to call me 'E-o.' 'Tis no me name, and it sounds foolish."

"Well, then tell me how to say it."

"Another time. When I feel the need to smile, I shall teach

ye. There is too much sorrow in me heart now to do so. And I willna tell ye, lass. I'll leave it to Baodan to do so should he feel the need."

I rolled my eyes and stood to leave him to Rhona to care for him. I loved Baodan and I liked Eoghanan, but I couldn't stand the mindset that they both seemed to have. Their belief that a man needed to decide where I should stay or what I should hear. Besides, I already knew what he was talking about.

"There's no need for Baodan to tell me. I already know that Niall had something to do with your mother's illness and with what happened to Griogair, though I'm not sure Baodan realizes it yet. The only thing I don't know is why. If you do know and you'd like to tell me, I'd love to hear it. If not, it's no matter. I'm pretty resourceful. I doubt it will take me very long to figure it out. Now, eat some food, and take a bath."

Leaving him gawking after me, I moved past him on the stairwell and went in the direction Rhona pointed out to me.

* * *

The darkness of the room forced me to retreat back into the hallway to find a torch to light the many candles scattered about. Once illuminated, I found it far less dusty than expected. Kenna had already done most of the dirty work.

I moved slowly about the room, glancing at the neat piles of books, trying to get my bearings as to how she divided things up. Trouble was, many of the books were not written in English. I slowly realized that I would be rather useless in categorizing the books.

With the promise of staying busy shattered, I sat down at the desk placed in the center of the space. One book lay open, encased in leather and filled with pages larger than any standard sheet of paper in present time. I found it to be beautiful, mysterious, and as I flipped through the pages covered in writing, I stopped at the sight of words I recognized.

Surprisingly, and quite unlike the other volumes scattered throughout the room, it was not written in Gaelic. The hand was in English, and it was not a book at all but a journal.

Whose, I didn't know, but there were limited possibilities. Baodan didn't strike me as the type to pour his feelings onto the page, neither did Niall. Eoghanan seemed a possibility, but the words looked too feminine. Although written in English, the flourished, cursive handwriting made for difficult reading.

My next guess was Kenna, but I wasn't sure how common it was for women to read during this time. Perhaps, being lady of a castle provided one with more education.

I started at the beginning, taking note of the first date written over eight years prior. Scanning the pages, I flipped to the last entry only a little more than halfway through the journal. The last time someone had put pen to the page of the diary sitting before me was seven years ago, and the last entry read very dark indeed.

Kenna didn't write these words. Only one person could have written something so morbid.

Baodan's late-wife, Osla.

Chapter 30

Cameron Castle

"Ye are no going back inside until I have spoken to ye." Baodan grabbed Niall by the arm, dragging him effortlessly to the side of the castle, away from the burial. He wished to squeeze his arm until the bone snapped, to beat the wretch until his fists were covered in his brother's blood.

"I'm afraid I doona have time, brother. There is much to be done. With Aunt Nairne still missing, there is none to assist them but me. Believe me, I now understand what it must be like for ye all the time. I doona envy yer position."

Niall tried to jerk from his grasp, but Baodan held him tightly, bringing his face in close so that none could hear his words but Niall. "Doona behave as if ye have done no wrong. If ye hadna, ye would have greeted me as soon as I arrived, no pretend as if ye dinna know me."

Baodan didn't miss the shift in Niall's gaze, the darkness that cascaded over them as he changed his demeanor. Malice festered in his brother's eyes that he'd not ever noticed before.

"The only wrong I have done is try to bed yer whore, but she is an ungrateful bitch who should be taught no to bite the hands that feed her."

His fist hit Niall's side with enough force to crack a rib. Baodan held his brother upright to keep him from doubling over in pain. It wouldn't do for anyone to notice the tension between them. None needed to be aware of what he planned for Niall. Not until he knew all that his brother had been up to.

"She is no a whore. She is a permanent member of yer former home. Doona dare show yer face there again, for ye willna be welcome."

Shock spread across Niall's face as he inhaled deeply and stood as upright as he could. "McMillan Castle is no more yer home than mine, but 'tis no matter. I have been welcomed here with open arms. It shall be many a year until Griogair's son is old enough to take over the duties here."

"'Twould be a mistake for ye to get comfortable in yer position here. I will no more allow ye to care for this territory than I would allow ye to care for me own. Do ye think that I doona see what ye have done here?" Baodan released his grip on his brother and forced a smile at one of the castle maids who walked by. Watching until she was out of view, Baodan grabbed onto him once more.

"Just what is it that ye think I have done?"

A jest lay within Niall's gaze, a dare for Baodan to tell him what he knew his brother didn't know. It infuriated Baodan that Niall was right. He didn't understand all that had happened but, as he stared down the evil within his brother's eyes, he knew who to blame. "I doona know how, and I sure canna see why, but I believe Griogair's death came by yer hand."

"Me hand?" Niall's angry voice dripped with sarcasm as he glared disdainfully back at Baodan. "I can swear to ye that I no laid a hand on him. I rather liked our dear cousin."

"I believe that ye dinna lay a hand on him, but 'twas yer poison killed him, and it wasna the first time ye have used such a potion."

"Oh? And who else do ye think I have killed? Have ye no spent yer entire life side by side with me? Doona ye think ye would have noticed if I was capable of murder?"

Baodan shook his head. "No, I remained too blind, too wrapped up in me own selfish pity to see right in front of me. I doona know who else ye have killed, but I do know who ye have tried to. Eoghanan was right to get Mother out of yer reach."

"Ach, Baodan. What reason would I have for hurting her? 'Tis no secret that I despise her, but what would I have to gain from her death?

"I doona know, but everything ye do is for yer own gain, so I know there must be a reason."

Baodan stilled at the smile that spread across his brother's face. Niall finished his jest, enjoying the freedom of not having to hide his hatred.

"Ah, so Eoghanan has said nothing then? O'course he hasna. I can tell by the look on yer face that ye know nothing, and I believe that ye never shall. The bastard is too honorable, too caring to hurt ye in such a way."

Baodan closed his eyes and breathed deeply, picturing the lass that awaited him at home. He could not kill his brother here, not until he rallied enough forces to push Niall away from Cameron Castle. Away from all that he held dear. "I willna ask ye what ye mean, for it would bring ye pleasure, and ye are deserving of none. Enjoy yer time as Laird, for it shan't last long, brother." Baodan dropped his hand from Niall's arm, turning so that he could mount his horse.

"Will it no? I doona see how ye shall end it. I will tell ye this and 'tis the truth whether ye wish to hear it or no. Griogair was no the person I wished to harm."

Baodan turned to look at Niall over his shoulder. "Do ye think me a fool, Niall? I know that he wasna the one ye aimed for. Ye told many that ye were headed to see Mother, dinna ye? And 'twas Mother's food that ye believed ye'd poisoned."

Niall laughed, and the sound of it chilled Baodan to his bones.

"Aye, but it seems that all has turned out for the best. With Griogair gone, I now have a home when ye have denied me one."

"And what of Nairne, did ye kill her as well?"

"No, 'tis all that troubles me, for I doona know where she is. I expect she is dead somewhere on the castle grounds. Felled by the grief of watching her only son die before her eyes. But believe me, if she is no dead, I shall be the first to find her, and the last to see her alive."

Baodan needed to leave here, to return home to find the truth that he sought and to wrap his arms around the woman he loved. Yet he had to find a way to protect his aunt. His heart filled with enough hate and disgust to last a lifetime, and he needed to wash it away before it consumed him. "Do ye think that Nairne's words are all that can end ye? I doona need proof of what I know for men to join me against ye. Me word is worth much more than yer own." Baodan turned but he heard Niall's snickers as he walked away.

"And just what makes ye think that?"

Baodan kept his back to his brother as he spoke, moving away from the monster behind him. "While I have denied meself much, I havena spent me life treating others like they are mine to pawn as I wish. I have many a friend, while ye have none. There is more power that lies in that than ye know."

For the first time in as long as Baodan could remember, his brother said nothing. Baodan rode away from Cameron

Castle knowing he must rally his forces with all speed, or he wouldn't be able to protect his aunt.

All he could hope was Niall had taken his bait and would come after him before finding Nairne. Surely Niall would be more concerned with stopping him than finding their helpless aunt.

Chapter 31

Every instant spent within Osla's journals brought me closer to her secret. Unable to continue the work Kenna started, I offered to help Rhona in the kitchens but made sure to sneak away for a few hours each afternoon so that I could dive into Osla's sad world.

Eoghanan remained absent after the first day, but I knew he stayed around the castle. Each day on my way to the tower room, I would see him pacing outside, waiting with baited breath for Baodan's return.

The seventh morning after Baodan's departure, I woke early and headed straight for the tower room. We expected Baodan back today, and I wanted to finish the few entries left in Osla's book. With every step up to the room, I prayed that the answer would reveal itself in the riddles gone unsolved for far too long.

The book detailed her gentle descent into darkness and the evolution from happiness to despair broke my heart. Osla's life had been a happy one, at least for a while.

> *"After much begging, Eoghanan agreed to teach me to write. Baodan would have taught me, but he would not have understood my desire to learn as Eoghanan has. He too holds things within and finds release within the written word. We have worked for many months, and I have left these pages empty until*

*I was skilled enough to grace them. Finally, he
says I am ready and now, when I am too quiet
to speak, I will pour out my soul to these
empty pages."*

I wondered if Baodan knew that Eoghanan taught her.
Their lessons must have begun even before they married for
she detailed the wedding.

*"Today shall be wondrous. Even if clouds fill
the sky, there will be sun in my heart."*

I flipped past those entries. The girl seemed likeable
enough, but I didn't really want to read about how madly in
love she'd been with the man I loved. Dead or not, the thought
caused jealousy to flare within me.

Her entries continued happily for the first five days of my
search but, on the sixth day, her words took a turn for the
worse and with them, a secret of betrayal uncovered.

*"He is the devil, yet I am drawn to him. I
know that what he offers I should not take, yet
I am tempted."*

Two entries later, guilt and despair.

*"I have betrayed the man I love most in all of
the world, all for a moment in the arms of evil.
I was a fool. 'Twas empty compared to the
love I receive from Baodan. I should not have
listened to his sweet words. I have seen too
many lasses enter and leave his bed, why did I
believe that I was different to him? I deserve
the hell that awaits me."*

She never mentioned the man's name, not that she needed to. Only one person within the castle fit her description. Niall.

I sat down on day seven, picking up on the aftermath of their affair. Baodan knew nothing of this, but I suspected Eoghanan kept it from his brother. A few entries down the page, my suspicions were confirmed.

> *"I wish this to end, but Niall threatens me, and so I must obey. Today our secret was discovered. Eoghanan saw us together. I could not be filled with more shame. There is perhaps some good that has come from his discovery. He will not allow Niall to touch me again. Upon finding us, he covered me and tore Niall from the bed, smashing him into the wall. He told him that if he ever came to me again, he would kill him. It was not an idle threat, and I believe that Niall knows that."*

I understood why Eoghanan had not told Baodan. He cared very much for Osla. He knew her regret and didn't wish to dishonor her. He also understood Baodan well enough to know that the knowledge would destroy him. So he kept their secret, not foreseeing the trouble that would arise from it.

> *"I am grateful that Eoghanan will keep my secret, but I can bear it no longer. Tonight, I will tell Niall my wish to confess. Perhaps, he will see reason and we can tell Baodan of our betrayal together."*

I'd spent very little time with Niall, and even I knew that would never work. Only one entry remained, and it differed from all of the rest. So hopeless were the words, even the handwriting changed. While I knew not the exact date of Osla's death, I knew her life ended shortly after these words. This Osla bore no resemblance to the one who started the journal.

> *"Secrets lead to death and I will welcome mine. Then Baodan will be free of me."*

If the entry ended there, suicide would have been a believable death, but the words that followed proved the key to the true secret behind it all.

> *"I should end my life but I am too much of a coward, too selfish to release Baodan of me. Despite my agony, the will to live is strong. Although I try to diminish its flame, there is a spark of hope within me. Hope that my mind will heal itself, but I know that I will not be given the time to do so. He comes for me, I feel it every moment, and fear has taken up permanent residence within my heart. My moments left in this world are few, and perhaps, that is just as it should be."*

I sat blinking at the empty pages following her words as I put together all of the pieces within my mind. Osla hadn't killed herself as Baodan believed. She'd been murdered by the same man who tempted her into his bed, making the rest of her brief life a living hell.

A few pieces still lay unconnected. Eoghanan's illness on the night of Osla's death, Kenna's sickness that caused her to leave McMillan Castle, and Griogair's sudden death now.

They all related to Osla.

I looked at the flickering light that danced on the walls around me. Slowly they seemed to ignite a light within me. Kenna worked within this very room before falling ill, saw the very words sitting before me. Suddenly, I could see it all.

As each piece fell smoothly into place, a voice behind me jerked me out of my thoughts.

I turned to see Eoghanan standing in the doorway.

"Ye canna tell him, lass. No ever."

Chapter 32

"Why?" I wanted nothing more than to tell Baodan. He deserved to know the truth after believing himself at fault for so many years. More than that, he needed to know.

Eoghanan moved inside the room, leaning against the desk in front of me as he closed Osla's journal. "There is no need for him to know. 'Twould only cause him pain."

"He's already in pain." I stood, confused and frustrated. "Keeping the truth from someone doesn't protect them. It only keeps them living a lie longer than they need to. Baodan blames himself for what happened to her. He thinks he wasn't enough to make her happy."

Eoghanan regarded me skeptically. "How could he think such? Osla loved him more than anyone."

"He thinks that because Baodan thinks everything is his fault."

"To tell him would only lay the blame with Osla and 'tis no her fault either."

"Bullshit."

I pressed my fingers hard against my forehead, willing myself not to lose it in a show of anger. I couldn't take another moment of this "women are weak" mindset that all of these men seemed to have.

"I'm sure you've never heard the expression, but it takes two to tango. Niall is at fault more than anyone, but unlike he tried to do with me, I don't get the impression that Niall forced Osla into his bed. We have our own minds, and we are responsible for our own choices. I know that you liked her, but she played a part in this. I'm not saying that she doesn't deserve forgiveness, but better Baodan lay the blame on her and Niall than on himself a moment more."

For a long while, Eoghanan paced the room as he started to speak, only to stop after a few syllables. "Ye...ye...I..."

I could take no more. "Oh gracious, just spit it out!"

"Ye are the oddest lass I have ever seen."

"Yeah, I get that a lot around here." I crossed my arms as I glared back at him. We stood in an odd sort of showdown across the tower room. Him at one end gripping the journal, me in front of the doorway blocking his exit.

"I mean it, lass. I've never heard a woman speak the way that ye do."

"Am I wrong?"

He placed the journal back on the table, and I took it as a sign of his resignation. "Ye are no wrong. 'Tis only that I havena spoken of all that happened in so long, it pains me to do so now."

"I'm sorry. I shouldn't have been so harsh." Of course it hurt him. The death of his friend, the grief of Baodan, the betrayal of Niall. Too much for anyone to keep inside of them for so long. "Why did you? Why haven't you told anyone?"

I stepped outside the door and waved for Eoghanan to join me out on the steps. He nodded and followed, only speaking once we were both seated.

"For the longest time, I dinna see it, what Niall had done. I suppose I dinna really want to. She couldna move past what she'd done, couldna bear the guilt of it. It wasna so difficult to believe that she would harm herself."

He stared in front of him and, although he spoke to me, Eoghanan's mind roamed far away, lost in dark memories of the past. I allowed him his silence until he readied himself to speak again.

"After her death, I could think of no good reason to tell Baodan about the affair. He dinna need any more pain, and Niall had already done all of the damage he could. I was wrong to think so, but I thought 'twould be best to leave their secret in the past."

"How long did you believe she ended her own life? When did you learn what Niall had done?"

"'Twas only after our mother fell ill. She would never tell me, but I knew by the way she started to treat Niall that she'd uncovered his secret. Shortly after, she fell ill. It dinna take long for me to see the similarities in her sickness and the one that felled me the night Osla died. 'Twas much slower moving, but she couldna eat nor hardly move from her bed. That's when I knew what he'd done."

"He killed Osla." I didn't ask it as a question. I knew what he would say.

"Aye. Niall would do anything to keep Baodan from learning what he had done. He knew that I dinna wish to tell him, but Mother would see it differently. Like ye, she would see the need for Baodan to know the truth. He killed Osla for the same reason. In the end, she wished to tell Baodan the truth, but he refused to give her the chance."

"So why not tell Baodan the truth once Kenna fell ill? Surely that concerned you enough to make you not worry about how the news might hurt him?"

He closed his eyes and I could sense the regret he tried to push away.

"I should have, lass. 'Tis the verra first thing I should have done, but I dinna trust him. Ye have changed him more than ye know, Mitsy. Before ye found him, Baodan blamed me as much as himself. I thought that if I approached him without proof, he would cast me aside for good. 'Tis why I sent our mother away, so that she would be safe until I found the proof I needed to approach Baodan."

Listening to his words, the final piece clicked into place. "But Niall went after her anyway, didn't he? He didn't mean to kill Griogair. He tried for your mother."

He nodded and glanced somberly in my direction. "Aye and 'tis me fault that Griogair is dead. Before I sent Mother away, I finally got the truth from her. She found the journal just as ye have done. She promised not to tell Baodan right away, to give me time to gather proof. Had I told Baodan sooner, Griogair would not have met such a fate. I doona believe that Niall truly wishes to be Laird, but the mishap provided him a convenient place to hide."

I reached out to him, wishing that he would understand through the squeeze of my hand just how wrong he was.

"There is no one to blame for Griogair's death but Niall. It's impossible to always see what the right choice is. You did your best with the knowledge you had. Of course you would expect that Baodan wouldn't believe you without proof. He has treated you poorly for far too long. He knows that now."

"Does he? I doubt it verra much, lass."

Eoghanan carried just about as much self-loathing as Baodan. It broke my heart to see it in both of them. "He does, I know he does because he told me."

"If he did, lass, then ye canna know how much he must love ye. For he never speaks to anyone about himself."

"Well, I'm pretty good at extracting information." I nudged him playfully, and a slight smile showed at the corner of his mouth, disappearing as quickly as it came.

"Aye, ye are that, and I see that ye are right. As soon as Baodan returns, we shall tell him. All has been kept secret for far too long. With Griogair's death, Niall must be stopped."

"Ye doona need to wait another moment for me to arrive. I think it best if ye both start speaking at once."

Either his footsteps were quiet or we were too engrossed in conversation, but neither of us noticed his approach until he stood before us. Tired, anxious, and scowling, Baodan moved past us on the stairwell and into the tower room.

Chapter 33

"Well…" he stood with his arms crossed, waiting for us to join him inside the room. Exhausted and dirty from his journey, it would have been understandable for him to be testy anyhow, but I knew that seeing Niall at the burial played a large part in Baodan's cool greeting.

"Hey," Looking up, I gave him a half-smile as I approached. Standing on my tip-toes once I was in front of him, I kissed him gently.

He thawed instantly and exhaled loudly as he squeezed me tight against him. I expected the breath had been awaiting escape for days.

"I'm sorry, lass. I am so pleased to see ye, but me soul is sick. I am tired of all these untruths. If either of ye know something that I doona, please for the love o'God, tell me now."

No matter the stress that hung in the air, I found it heaven to clutch onto him, to know he stood near me and not within Niall's reach. "Sit down. I'll tell you, and so will Eoghanan. The story isn't really mine."

* * *

As Eoghanan stepped forward, I leaned against the wall allowing the brothers their moment of revelation, never tearing my gaze from Baodan's stony face. I knew the ache that started deep in your stomach and spread after the betrayal of a spouse. The difference was, Baodan loved Osla where I never truly loved Brian, not in the way that one should. It would be even harder for Baodan.

The revelation of all Niall had done seemed expected, I could see it in his eyes that Baodan now knew the evil that lay within his brother. Osla's betrayal would be what stopped him cold. And it did.

"No." Baodan stood and took an angry step in Eoghanan's direction. "I know that I wasna fair to ye after she died, and I canna apologize to ye enough. I know that 'twas no yer fault, but I willna allow ye to speak such lies against her."

Eoghanan glanced at me sideways, and my heart squeezed uncomfortably at the hurt I knew Eoghanan felt at his brother's lingering mistrust. I stepped out of the shadows and pointed at the table where the journal lay. "Baodan, don't. He has no reason to lie to you. It's right there."

He turned and looked down at the closed book, raising his hands in frustration. "What's this?"

"It's hers," I said softly. I didn't want him to read it, but I knew he would not believe it otherwise.

"No. She dinna know how to write, nor read."

"Aye, she did, Baodan. I taught her meself."

Baodan's clenched fists showed the only sign that he heard Eoghanan's words. Hesitantly he flipped open the worn cover. Every bit of me wished I could prevent the pain coming to him.

* * *

Much time passed, and I couldn't breathe with the anticipation of his reaction.

When he spoke, anguish filled his cracked voice. "'Twas Niall. He killed her, dinna he?"

Red eyes brimming with unshed tears faced us as Baodan

turned from his seat. I wanted to run to him and throw my arms around him, but I couldn't bring myself to do so. This pain stemmed from a time before me, and he didn't want me near him in this instant.

"Aye, but 'twas only after Mother fell that I learned the truth meself." Eoghanan took one step toward his brother but stopped as Baodan held up his hand. He wished distance from us both.

"Ah, 'tis why ye sent her away?"

"Aye."

Baodan stood, his eyes moving back and forth between me and Eoghanan. The pain etched on his face hurt me to my core.

"Thank ye for telling me. If ye will excuse me, I should like to be alone."

"I'm afraid ye doona have time for that, sir. The entire Conall clan along with yer mother has just arrived at yer door." All of our heads turned in unison to see the hurried maid scurry back down the stairwell.

Baodan nodded and stepped toward the doorway. "'Tis good that they have come. We shall need them. Rally the keep and make ready for trouble. It comes."

"Ye stay as long as ye need, Baodan. I'll go and see all is done." Eoghanan assured him as he waved him back.

I stood still until Eoghanan retreated, but I could refrain myself no longer, whether he wanted it or not. I needed to touch Baodan. "I know you want to be alone and I'll leave you in just a moment, but I...I need you to know that I'm here."

One lone tear spilled out of his eyes, and I reached my thumb up to brush it away. He grabbed my hand and held my palm against his face, not trying to hide the pain. It meant more to me than he realized.

"I'm verra glad for it, lass, for I feel quite out of sorts with the world."

"That's okay, you don't always have to be so strong."

He placed his own palm against my face and pulled me close, stroking my hair with his fingers. "Aye, today I do, lass, but there is none that gives me strength the way that ye do."

Chapter 34

No longer within Niall's reach, Kenna would no longer keep her silence. Otherwise, I could see no reason for her to bring all of the Conalls with her on her return home. Yet Baodan seemed glad that she brought so many. She knew the support of many clans would be needed to end Niall.

Walking hand-in-hand, Baodan and I made our way down to the castle entrance. I grew more nervous with each step. For if the clans gathered, it meant battle approached.

"I wish I'd used a knife on him instead of my hands," I said.

"What did ye say?"

"Oh." I hadn't realized I'd even uttered the thought out loud. "Um…I said, I wished I'd used a knife on him that night. Then he'd already be dead."

"Ach, lass." Baodan continued moving but looked down at me in shock. "I am verra glad ye did no such thing. If ye had succeeded, ye wouldna be able to deal with the killing of a man. Ye are too soft-hearted."

"Pssh." The sound escaped as I rolled my eyes. I'd love the opportunity to knife the sick asshole.

"Oh, me God. She's alive." Baodan pulled away from me and ran across the main entryway, scooping up a woman I assumed to be his aunt into his arms.

I stayed back, allowing them a moment, smiling in relief that she eluded Niall's grasp.

I heard her approaching before I saw her. The quick, hurried step and fast voice a sure sign that Adelle came my way. I looked to my left to see all of my favorite girls approaching, accompanied by a shockingly attractive older gentlemen who had to be Adelle's husband.

"Oh. My. Gosh." I mouthed the words, emitting no sound as she passed, grinning like a schoolgirl. I turned my head to follow her and held up my hands in question.

"I know." My best friend's mother's words were a high, happy screech, and she latched on to my arm in her delight. "This…" we turned in unison, "is my husband, Hew."

I extended a hand in his direction and he took it gladly, his giant hand swallowing my own. "It's very nice to meet you. You must be quite something to have wrangled in Adelle."

He laughed a deep, friendly laugh, and his smile reached his eyes. The best smiles, from the kindest people, always did.

"Ach, I am verra pleased to meet ye. I have heard much about ye."

"Oh no." I laughed as I shook his hand, unable to draw my attention away from his beautiful brown eyes and shortly cropped hair. He stood out from all the other men in this time, and it suited him.

"All good things." He retracted his hand and nodded before turning to leave us, sensing, I suppose, our desire to talk about him.

"Adelle, you hooked a good one." I tried to whisper, but so tickled with the shock of seeing her so settled, my attempt at a whisper failed. Both Bri and Blaire laughed and scooted in closer to join the conversation.

"I think somebody's got a little crush, Mom."

Bri winked at me, and I reached out to run the side of my hand across little Ellie's sleeping face. She looked beautiful with a baby in her arms.

"Oh, give me a break. It's just that I'm happy for her is all. I'm happy for all of you."

"Ditto." Bri lifted the baby and nudged her head in the direction of the staircase. "Will you show me where I can lay her? Then, we can all resume our visiting while Baodan and the men sit down to their planning."

"Yes, of course." Together we walked up the staircase. "What did Kenna tell all of you?"

"Most everything, I think."

Bri didn't seem overly worried, which was very odd, but it did help to calm my anxious nerves. Motherhood suited her.

"Kenna said she told you two she was coming to see the baby, but she was really coming to ask for our assistance. I suppose she didn't want to tell Baodan at the time. She wanted him at home to watch over McMillan Castle and, if he's anything like the Conall men, he would have turned around to follow his mother had she told him."

"Yes." I nodded. "He would have."

"We were readying to leave when Nairne showed up, exhausted and sick from traveling by foot for days. She is grief stricken but mainly she's angry as hell. She watched her son die before her eyes, and she knew instantly Niall was to blame. Kenna told her all she knew before she headed our direction."

"God, I can't imagine. Witnessing the death of her son, unable to stop it, then dragging herself all the way here. It's terrible."

"Yes." The baby stirred in her arms, and she bent to kiss Ellie gently on the forehead before continuing. "All of it is, and he must be stopped. It's scary, you know, how you can spend time around someone and just never see who they really are. Granted, I've not spent much time with Niall, but I always thought him rather harmless."

I shivered at the thought of anyone thinking him harmless. Then again, I'd had a very different introduction to him than most. "No, that's not the word I would use to describe him. Here." I opened the door to Baodan's bedchamber. "You can put her in here."

I knew it to be much too early to know for sure, but I felt very different. As of late, the food here actually tasted good, and I found myself inexplicably dizzy at random times throughout the day. My body just felt weird.

I wanted to see what a sleeping babe looked like in the center of our bed. If my suspicions were correct, there'd be one joining us there soon enough.

Chapter 35

"Mitsy, lass, wake up."

Baodan's lips brushed my brow and I stirred, grinning into the blanket. I sat in a chair I moved next to the bed and only my top half lay on the blankets, my hand extended with Ellie's precious little fingers wrapped around one of mine.

"There is a visitor in me bed." He bent, wrapping his arms around me as his cheek pressed against my own, and I turned to kiss the side of his face.

"Yes. Bri needed to rest after the journey so I told her to leave Ellie with me, seems I needed to rest as well."

"Aye, ye look lovely next to a bairn."

"Hmm..." I wasn't certain, and I would tell him nothing until I was. "What's been decided?" Delicately pulling my finger from Ellie's grasp, I twisted in my seat and stood so that I pressed flat against him, my arms wrapped around his waist.

"We will leave in the morning. Me own men, along with the Conalls and many of their men. It should end easily, but I canna say for sure with Niall. I doona believe many at Cameron Castle will follow him should he try to stand against us, but he is cunning. He willna go without one of his games."

"What will you do with him?" I ran my hands up and down him, tickling his bare back with my fingertips. His week away seemed an eternity. I wanted nothing more than to stay with my arms wrapped around him forever.

"Kill him, lass. There is no other end for him. No more chance for redemption."

"I'm sorry. It shouldn't be that way. You shouldn't be

placed in that position, not with your own brother."

"No, but we all go through things we shouldna have to. Ye taught me that, lass. Ye have taught me many things."

I moved my hands to the side of his face and stretched to plant a kiss on his beautiful lips. "I don't know about that. You give me too much credit."

"No." He grabbed my face so that our positions mimicked one another. Suddenly, his eyes grew very serious. "I doona give ye enough. There is something I must tell ye, lass. Something I wished to say to ye many a night ago but 'twas interrupted. The words have been on me heart since that night, and I willna be able to breathe well until I have them said."

My skin covered itself in goosies as fireflies danced in my stomach. "What?" I grinned, my cheeks prevented from spreading wide by his hands on the side of my face.

"I love ye. Without doubt nor hesitation, none in me life has ever captured me heart as ye have."

"Surely not." I knew he loved me, but he didn't need to lie. I also knew the special place Osla occupied in his heart.

He shook his head, pressing his lips against me before speaking again. "Aye lass, surely so. I understand yer meaning and aye, even more than her. Osla was me wife and I did love her, but no like this. 'Twas only that before ye came to me, I dinna know that love could be any stronger than the love I had before. But, Mitsy, it can. I am hopeless against ye. 'Tis no only me heart that ye have captured, but me verra soul. Ye reside here," he tapped his chest, "and I intend to keep ye there forever."

Mr. Darcy himself, in the flesh, could not have beaten that speech. My eyes started watering and my lip trembled. I looked ridiculous and Baodan's face fell instantly.

"Have I upset ye, lass?"

"Oh, God no! It's just, well, gracious, what did you expect a girl to do with words like that? I love you too. You know that."

"Then marry me, lass. Tonight."

"Yes. I want nothing more."

I expected him to kiss me. Instead, he smiled and stepped abruptly away and spoke to the doorway. "Come in, lassies. She said aye."

"What?" My arms hung in the air, still hugging empty space. "Everybody already knows? Well, that was a gamble, wasn't it?"

He laughed and shook his head. "From yer reaction, I doona think that it was. I canna wait a moment longer, lass. If ye had said no, I doona know what I would have done, for all is ready except ye. I wish to be married to ye right away."

As exquisitely happy as I was in that moment, a part of me wondered if his hurry also had something to do with his plans for Niall.

Did Baodan fear that he might not return from his reckoning with his brother and wanted to give me the protection of his name and clan?

The thought put me very ill at ease.

Chapter 36

All gathered by the pond. The sun set in the distance, casting beautiful rays of light that bounced off the rippling water as it dipped into the horizon.

"Are ye ready, dear?" Kenna patted me as we locked arms, and I shook my head at the tears in her eyes

"No, you can't cry! I'm already about to lose it. If you cry, I'll cry, then I expect Baodan will cry. It simply won't do."

"Verra right, dear."

Kenna laughed and pulled away to sniffle and gather herself. When she returned to my side, her eyes were red but dry. As good as they were gonna get.

"I'm very fond of your son. I didn't think, I didn't expect to be doing this again."

Adelle started blubbering on the other side of me, and I forced myself to turn away from Kenna. "Oh no. Not you too. Go clean yourself up."

I whirled back to Kenna who laughed quietly. "We are a fair mess, are we no? I am verra glad that ye are fond of him. I am fond of him as well. And of ye, dear. I doona believe there has ever been two people more deserving of the other's affections."

"Thank you. I'm ready. Let's do this."

In a flash, Adelle returned to my side, fresh as a daisy.

As we started our walk toward the gathered group, I smiled, all nervousness gone.

* * *

Our eyes locked as I neared him. From that moment, nothing else in the world mattered but Baodan.

He reached for my hands, and the rest of the ceremony passed in a blur. I knew not what I said or how long it lasted, but I knew for sure it didn't matter at all. Only something so right could be so absorbing.

His kiss at the end came suddenly, and I melted against him as everyone erupted into cheers around us.

For all my chiding of Kenna and Adelle, my own tears flowed freely as we walked down the center of the crowd as husband and wife.

"Thank ye, lass." He bent and whispered in my ear.

"For what?"

"Ye have given me back what no man can live without. Love. And hope. Ye have given me back me hope, Mitsy, and I couldna love ye more for it. I'd die before I ever lived without ye from this day forward."

Chapter 37

"I think you must be part fish." I teased him at his suggestion that we have a bath brought up, clearly another set up for a water escapades of sorts.

"Part fish?" He wrapped his arms around my waist and nibbled playfully at my ear.

"Yes, water's great, but let's just get busy in the bed this time, not the water. I think my back is still bruised from those rocks."

"Get busy, lass? 'Tis like learning another language, listening to ye speak."

He worked at the laces of my dress, brushing my hair aside as he kissed the back of my neck.

"That's exquisite." I allowed my head to fall back against him, as my dress fell away.

He dropped his hands, drawing circles down my bare back with his thumbs. I tensed as he brushed over the tender spots about halfway down, and he immediately ceased the pressure. "Ach Mitsty, I am verra sorry, lass. 'Twas no me intention to cause ye harm."

"I know. You didn't cause me harm." I laughed at his dramatics. "It's just a couple of bruises."

"What was it ye told me that day? A kiss would make it better, aye?"

"Mmm...something like that." I arched against him as his lips trailed down my spine, his hands gripping my waist to keep him steady as he trailed downward.

He placed one light kiss on each small bruise then nipped

quickly at the highest part of my bottom. I yelped and squirmed away from him, but he grabbed me quickly, scooping me up as he carried me to the bed.

"Fine, I doona care where I bed ye in this moment. Whether it be in the water, or the bed, or before a crowd of onlookers, I want to fall asleep deep inside me wife."

"Eeek. I don't think your mother or your brother would enjoy that sort of show, so let's just keep it in the bedroom." I laughed as he threw me onto the bed, diving on top of me as he kissed me roughly.

I moaned as he bit my lower lip, keeping it in between his teeth as he tugged it toward him. It was deliciously painful, and I feared I might shatter beneath him even before he touched me.

I needed him inside me, to cling to him as I lost myself for the first time as his wife.

I said nothing, but he understood what I needed as I moved against him, and seconds after I removed his kilt, he slipped himself inside me.

The first time moved quickly, our need for each other too raw to stretch out our release. No matter, much night remained and, as the evening passed, we took advantage of every instant of our first night of betrothal, making love to one another until dawn.

Chapter 38

The next morning, Baodan left our bed early, and the carefree haze that covered the night before evaporated in an instant. Today, the men marched toward Cameron Castle.

Now cold and anxious without him near me, I dressed and went in search of Bri. I knew she wouldn't be able to confirm my suspicions, but I wanted to know if she'd exhibited similar symptoms while pregnant with Ellie.

I found her in the kitchen, kneading dough with Rhona, Blaire, and the Conall's beloved kitchen maid and boss of everyone, Mary.

"Hey there. Aren't you all glowing? Somebody didn't get much sleep."

Bri winked at me, and I blushed before stepping into the kitchen.

"'Tis just as it should be. No bride should sleep on her wedding night. Oh, how I wish I could go back to it, though I'm quite sure I doona remember how it all works." Mary laughed and stepped away from her perfect kneading loaf, dipping her hands in a cool bucket of water to rinse them.

"Bri, can I talk to you for a moment?"

She smiled and stepped away to rinse as Mary had done. She grabbed my arm as she stood next to me, concern evident on her face. "Is everything alright?"

I nodded but said nothing as I unconsciously glanced down at my stomach. Bri's eyes widened in understanding, and she bent to whisper to me. "Of course. Let's go."

As soon as I walked back into my bedchamber with Bri

trailing me, I spun to face her. "I know it's way too soon, but something just feels off. Different. How did you feel during the early stages of your pregnancy?"

Bri smiled and nodded, "Much the same. You won't know for certain for a few weeks, but I could sense a change within me days after I became pregnant. You'll have to wait and see, but I very much bet that you're right."

* * *

All men sat at the ready, awaiting Baodan's command that they begin their journey to Cameron Castle. Eoghanan knew not how Niall would try to evade him, but his brother would do his best to outsmart them all.

If Niall chose poison as his weapon once again, at least Eoghanan would now have the antidote at the ready. He only needed to retrieve it from his bedchamber. He spotted where he left it and swiftly snatched the precious liquid up.

He hurried back down the hallway, only stopping by chance outside Baodan's bedchamber as the vial slipped from his hands. He bent to grab the antidote that rolled right against the bedchamber door at the exact same moment that Bri's voice echoed inside the large room.

Niall had to die, now more than ever, for his new sister could be with child.

Chapter 39

"I doona wish for ye to be frightened, lass. All will be fine. I, along with all me men, shall return safely in a few brief days." Baodan squeezed my hands tightly as he bent to kiss me goodbye.

"I know. I'm not scared." He knew I lied, but thankfully he didn't contradict me. If I allowed myself to voice my worry, I'd fall apart.

"There will be guards all around the castle, but I doona want any of ye lassies to step outside the castle. Stay together when ye can. I expect no trouble here, but I need ye all to stay safe."

I nodded, hoping he would leave soon. The quicker they left, the sooner they could return. "We will. Now go." I reached up to kiss him again. "There's no point in delaying it. I love you."

"And I ye, lass."

He turned and mounted his horse. I looked for Eoghanan to bid him farewell but saw him missing from the group. "Where's E-o?"

"Right here, lass."

He approached me from behind, and I turned to throw my arms around him. "Stay safe, please."

He patted me gently on the back, and I stilled as he whispered in my ear. "Aye, I will. Ye do the same, lass. I know about the bairn."

I pulled away and stared at him with wide eyes. "What? How?"

He kept his voice low. I was thankful that Baodan was too far away to hear him. "I dinna mean to, but I heard Bri as she spoke to ye."

"Please, don't tell him. There's no way to know yet. I may not be pregnant. He doesn't need anything to distract him while he's gone. He would only worry."

He smiled, and I knew he understood. There were few men as intuitive or thoughtful as Eoghanan.

"I know, Mitsy. I only wished to ask ye to take care with yerself."

"Thank you. I will. Bring him back safely to me, okay?"

He turned to leave but glanced back at me as he spoke. "Aye, I swear to ye I will. There is nothing I would no do to protect either of ye."

Chapter 40

Heavy hearts filled the grand sitting room at McMillan Castle as soon as the men were gone. Each of us sat in silent prayer for the men we loved, each shallow breath a hope that all would return unharmed. The numbers were in our favor, as far as we knew, there were none at Cameron Castle who would deny them entry. Still, any time the threat of violence lingered, risk did as well.

Desperate to lighten the mood, I moved across the room to snatch tiny Ellie out of Bri's arms. "Come here to your Aunt Mitz. I want to squeeze those little cheeks of yours until you squeal with laughter." Squeal she did, the moment I put her in my arms, but not from delight.

"Alright, here you go. Just take a chill pill. I wasn't really going to squeeze your cheeks." Embarrassed and feeling foolish, I extended the screeching baby in her mother's direction while the rest of the room chuckled quietly. At least I succeeded in breaking the eerie silence. "I'm going to be rotten at this."

"What?"

The voice belonged to Adelle. She needed no further explanation to practically charge me from the other side of the room as she enveloped me into a hug tight enough to push the baby right out of me.

"You're having a baby?"

She squealed in my ears, which did nothing to calm the already upset Ellie.

"What?" Kenna's voice, much like Adelle's, echoed

throughout the room.

Before I could respond to either of them, I was squashed in between a grandmother sandwich. "No. Maybe. It's way too early to tell. I've said nothing to Baodan. I didn't mean to say anything now."

"What?" The same word, but said in a completely different tone as both women stepped away and glared at me disapprovingly. Kenna's eyes were about to bug out of her head. "Ye told us before ye told him. He will no be glad to hear it, lass."

I wasn't about to apologize for my decision to keep it quiet while he was away. I had no doubt they would have done the same. "I didn't mean to tell you. I just already spoke to Bri about the possibility and when Ellie went to screaming it just slipped out. And of course I didn't tell Baodan before he left. I don't even know if I am, and it would only serve to distract him. That's the last thing he needs."

"Aye, ye are right about that, dear." Kenna's eyes resumed their normal size as she ran her hand up and down my arm in a motherly fashion. "I havena been this happy in a verra long time."

"Don't be." I wanted to smack myself for speaking so loosely. "I don't know anything. I'm probably not."

"Oh girly." Adelle rushed me and threw one of her long arms around my shoulders, pressing her cheeks flat against mine. "If you really feel that you are, I expect it's true. Your body has its ways of telling you."

"Exactly." Bri winked at her mother as she teased her, bouncing Ellie up and down on her knee to soothe her.

Adelle directed me to sit next to her near the fire. "I know that I'm not really your mother, but I consider all three of you

220

girls," she looked around at me, Bri, and Blaire. "part mine. I'm thrilled that I may have another grandbaby coming. And don't you fret, Blaire. It will happen with time. When it's meant to."

Blaire smiled politely, but I could see doubt in her eyes. "I hope that ye are right, Adelle. I'm verra afraid that all the years I spent saying that I dinna want children have come back to punish me now that I do."

Adelle waved a hand in dismissal. "Oh sweetie, that's just not the way things work. Do you know how many people say they don't want children and end up with a hoard? Sometimes, it just takes time."

Mary, the Conalls' beloved cook and castle maid, spoke up. "Aye, and even if it doesna come, children will find ye that are no yer own but ye love them just as much as if they were. Kip and I werena able to have children, but Eoin and Arran are no less mine than if I pushed them out of meself."

"Have you tried to get in touch with Morna? I bet she'd be happy to help if she could." Surely the thought crossed her mind, but I wanted to say something. I felt bad for speaking so foolishly.

Blaire smiled genuinely and nodded, her eyes wide. "Aye, I'm sure she would help, and that is precisely why I doona wish to ask for it. I know the meddling lass too well. She would no only give me one but three at once if it pleased her. That wouldna please me at all."

All of us who knew Morna laughed and nodded in agreement, only stopping as Rhona entered carrying a tray of food. "'Tis no verra much, lassies, but I doona expect that any of ye have much of an appetite anyway. I dinna see the need to go to much of a fuss without the men here. Too much of the food would go to waste."

"Thank you. Where are all the other girls?" Despite the lifted morale that resulted in the talk of babies, a cool breeze of warning swept down the back of my neck, and I suddenly felt very uneasy.

"They are all sleeping together in me own cottage on the castle grounds. They should be locked up safely for the evening. I wouldna allow them to go far from me while the lads are away."

"Good." I waved her in so that she would move closer to us. "And you will stay here with us."

"If 'tis what ye wish, I shall." She placed the tray of food in the center of the room. It didn't take long before Adelle dug in, and shortly after the other women followed.

Before Rhona entered, I thought myself hungry, but appetite eluded me as the sense of unease seemed to grow within me. I sat back. As I cast my attention to the darkest corners of the room, my attention drew to Nairne for the very first time that evening.

She said nothing as the rest of us spoke, given no sign of congratulations during talk of the maybe-baby. I knew she was grief-stricken over the loss of her son, but still, it seemed to me that she stayed too quiet. Her chair set slightly away from the rest of the group, the back of it covered in darkness. The fire barely cast a light on her, but I could make little of her out from where I sat.

I stood. Something deep within me screamed for me not to take a step near her, but I knew that I must. No one else noticed my slow approach toward her. I had to drag my feet to continue. I stopped as soon as I stood close enough to see her.

The blood drained from my face as I looked into her eyes.

They were open, but cold. And she could not see me.

Chapter 41

His heart beat painfully in his chest. There was no choice but to go forward, to find his brother and end him before he could harm another person he loved, but a deep wrongness hung in the air. Each hoof step that brought him and all the men with him further away from McMillan Castle made Baodan more certain.

"Halt!" He screamed the word, yanking hard on his horse's reins.

"Baodan, what are ye doing? We doona need to be away any longer than we must. Let us ride and end all of this."

Her heart thumped loudly in his hears. Nothing else around him, not his brother's voice, nor the sound of horses whining at their sudden stop could overwhelm the sound of it. He yearned for Mitsy's presence whenever away from her, but only in his dreams did he sense her presence so completely, until now. She was frightened and in danger. He could sense it.

"Something is no right. I should have left ye with them. It wasna right of us to leave them alone."

Eoghanan put a hand up to hush the men behind him. "We dinna leave them alone. There are many guards in place outside the castle."

"Aye, but Niall knows the castle too well. He could get inside if he wished it." If only the beating in his ears would cease; each thump drove him further into panic.

"Do ye think it possible? Do ye have reason to believe

that he is no longer at Cameron Castle?"

"I doona know, but there is trouble at home. I canna tell ye how I know, but I do. As surely as I know me own name, I know it."

"What do ye want me to do? Just tell me. I'll do it."

A scream in the distance in front of them prevented Baodan from answering his brother's question. A rider approached quickly, a woman. Griogair's widow.

"Baodan!" She screamed his name through the trees. The panic in her voice only heightened his fear.

"Go! Ride back home. For God's sake keep her safe. I canna lose her, Eoghanan. I'll follow ye shortly."

Eoghanan turned and nudged his horse until he galloped into the distance. By the time Baodan could no longer see him, Wynda was by his side.

"Did ye ride here alone? Ye shouldna have done so."

"Aye, I verra well should have. Doona move any further toward Cameron Castle. Niall isna there. None would join him to stand against ye, and he fled four days ago."

"Four days?" Baodan's ears rang with shock. He gripped tight on the reins to hold himself upright. It took only three days to reach Cameron Castle.

"Aye, and he headed here. I left as soon as I could, but he is a faster rider than I."

Baodan turned to his cousins who stood ready for his orders behind him. "Eoin, Arran, we must return to McMillan Castle at once. I shall ride ahead. See to Wynda's safety."

His entire world lay inside the walls of his castle. To think that Niall stood within reach of Mitsy filled him with enough rage to blind him. He wished to kill his monster of a brother. And kill him he would.

* * *

McMillan Castle

"Nairne. Nairne." I tried to say her name, but it came out as a breathless scratch; the very embodiment of nightmares, when the dreamer tries to scream and cannot. "Nairne!" Finally her name found its way past my trembling lips. When not a muscle within her twitched, I knew that she sat dead.

Everyone behind me still chatted busily, nibbling away at the meek meal. Slowly I moved to grip her arm. Warm to the touch, she'd not been dead long. At first glance, I thought perhaps her heart failed or a stroke killed her, but across her brown dress a patch of red spread, seeping its way through the thick fabric as it crawled across her torso.

Shaking, I took a step backward and tumbled, scrambling to get away from her in horror as I noticed the point of a blade protruding through her stomach.

A deep laugh started from behind the chair as I fell and, as everyone in the room hushed, Niall emerged from behind Nairne's lifeless body.

Chapter 42

No one screamed as Niall stepped from behind the chair, all of us too frozen with fear to move. His normally smooth and cocky appearance was gone. He looked utterly mad with his curly dark hair sticking up in every direction, his sick smile spread wide.

Every tooth in his head showed as he cackled uncontrollably. Slowly, I reined in my terror. Fear would hinder me. I'd stopped him once before. I would do so again.

We outnumbered him easily, and it was a room filled with intelligent, spitfire women. He was fool to approach us while we were grouped together.

"Ach, ye are one ugly bastard. Ye have no place here, and if ye so much as touch one red hair on Mitsy's head, I shall charge ye and sit on yer head until it bursts."

I glanced back at Mary in utter shock. Brunette or not, that old broad was a red-head at heart. She gave me a run for my money in the sass department.

"Hush, Mary." Bri reached to latch on to the old woman's hand, warning in her voice.

Niall laughed even more loudly before thrusting the sword out into the air in Mary's direction. "Ye best shut yer mouth, or I shall run this through it. I mean none of ye any harm. Me business is with this one."

He jerked his head toward me, and I stood for the first time since tripping.

"No harm? Son, ye killed her. Yer own aunt, and ye laugh at the sight of it. Have ye no caused enough pain? 'Tis over, ye have to know that." Kenna sobbed, her entire body shaking at the shock of her murderous child.

"Ach, Mother. Ye are verra right, there has been much pain caused by me, but doona worry, I'm nearly done. I know that I am no long for this world. Me brothers will end me, but before they do, I shall tear one more lass from Baodan's grasp. If ye doona wish to join her in death, then ye willna speak to me again."

She said nothing for the moment, and I took the opportunity to step into his line of sight. "Niall, she's not going to say anything else. It's just me and you, okay? I guess you're pretty angry, huh? For what I did to you?"

Nothing in me accepted that he would hurt me. I simply wouldn't allow it. One sword other than the one Niall held in his hands lay against the fireplace. If I could get him talking, I hoped to signal to Adelle who sat closest to sword. It needed to be in one of our hands.

"Aye, lass, I am verra angry indeed and, 'tis reason enough for me to kill ye, but 'tis no why I will take great pleasure from doing so."

"No? Then why?" Too riled up, Niall didn't notice the footsteps that approached the doorway, and I swallowed a sigh of relief at Eoghanan's shadow in the doorway.

His finger moved across his lips, signaling for me not to give away his presence.

"Why? Because Baodan has taken a fancy to ye, and it wouldna please me to allow him happiness."

"Has Baodan wronged you in some way? I thought it was you who did the wrong."

He threw his head back before scoffing at the question.

I put one hand behind my back and thrust my fingers in

the direction of the sword. I had no way of knowing whether my gesture would be noticed. With Eoghanan in the doorway, I hoped it would be less necessary.

"Has he wronged me? He has, though I doona believe he would ever see it that way. Osla's love for Baodan killed her, no me."

"Hmm...how do you figure?"

"If she dinna love him, then she would have kept our little secret, but she insisted that we tell him. At the time, I couldna allow it. So, ye see, she gave me no choice. The fault in that lies with Baodan."

"Gah, you are one twisted, sick, son of a bitch." I shook my head in disgust. Eoghanan needed to step in the room soon.

"Enough!" Niall moved forward quickly stopping when the point of his sword pressed into the center of my chest. "Eoghanan, I know ye are there. I am no the fool that ye all seem to think. Come out, or I shall run her through."

Eoghanan stepped quickly from the shadows, his face white with worry, his jaw clenched tight. "Niall, if ye hurt her, I swear I shall kill ye."

"Ye will kill me anyway, but I will no kill her right away. I will wait until Baodan arrives. I would verra much like for him to watch her die."

His eyes glinted with madness. "And now so must you."

Chapter 43

With the end of his sword pressed against me, I did as he bid, stepping into him. He dropped his sword as he wrapped one arm around my waist and withdrew a dirk tucked away inside his kilt. He pressed it into the flesh of my neck, pushing hard enough to draw blood.

I was rash and stupid to have assumed that he would be unable to hurt me. He did a fine job of it now. I couldn't die here, not like this. Not in the first place to ever feel like home, with a child possibly growing inside me.

Sobs threatened to overtake me but I knew if I did so, he would only push the blade deeper into my skin. Sound suddenly filled the hallway outside of the room, and Baodan charged inside, Eoin, Arran, and Hew with him.

In that instant I saw my own death, the pressure of the knife against my neck such that I truly believed he would draw it across me at that moment. I believe he almost did, but Baodan's voice stopped him.

"'Tis no Mitsy that ye wish to see dead. Doona take yer hatred of me out on another. No one else need die when 'tis truly me that ye wish to see dead. Release her and ye may run yer sword through me. I willna stop ye."

"No, Baodan, please." The words sent the knife deeper into my neck, but I couldn't remain silent. I couldn't allow him to die for me.

For the first time since entering the room, he looked me in the eyes. The pain and sorrow there sent tears streaming down my face. "Mitsy, lass, I canna lose ye. If I wasna to die now and ye were killed, 'twould no be long before I would follow ye in death. The grief of losing ye would kill me."

How could he not see that he would kill me anyway? As soon as Baodan was dead, Niall would turn his sword on me. An oath meant nothing to him. "No." My word was only a whisper, and he paid it no mind.

"But ye are stronger than me, lass. Ye have a spirit that canna be starved. Use the rock to return to yer home once I am gone and live a life filled with all the things ye wish for."

Niall said nothing throughout Baodan's speech, only stared in his brother's direction, his stare dark and unreadable.

"Niall. Let her go. To kill her will serve no purpose. With me gone, McMillan territory will be yers."

Niall's grip on my throat lessened. The idea appealed to him. Too lost in the thralls of his madness, he couldn't see the impossibility of Baodan's words. Niall remained surrounded at every side. Regardless of who died here, me, Boadan, or both of us, Niall would meet his end. Not a soul in the room planned on allowing him to live past sunrise. Baodan knew this too, which meant he played his brother. He didn't intend to let Niall kill either one of us.

When he finally spoke, I startled at the sound of Niall's voice in my ears, and he laughed at my show of nerves. "I will accept yer offer, brother, but I willna run ye through with me sword. If I tried to approach ye, I would be bested, and I will see ye dead." He squeezed the arm around my waist to get my attention and whispered angrily in my ear. "Reach behind ye, lass, and grab the vial tucked beneath the edge of me kilt. Toss it in Baodan's direction."

Poison. My hand trembled as I moved it. I reached for Baodan's death, for I knew he would drink it to save me. As much as I wished to crush the vial in my hand, I knew it would result in my immediate death. "Promise me, you'll let me go as soon as he drinks it. Allow me the chance to say goodbye."

"Fine. Throw it to him now."

Baodan caught it with ease, despite my shaky throw. He didn't wish to think about it, and he smiled as he popped the top. "I love ye more than ye will ever know, lass."

I sobbed as he downed the vile contents, screaming as he dropped to the floor. I no longer cared about the knife at my throat. Raising my arm, I threw my elbow deep into Niall's ribs and, as the knife fell away, I rushed to Baodan's side.

* * *

His body shook in convulsions, and his eyes rolled up into his head as I sobbed against him. When he stilled in my arms, Niall laughed ecstatically. Rage exploded within me. Reaching, I grasped onto the sword that lay to my right and stood to charge him.

He moved quickly when he saw me. Before I could stand, I saw the edge of his sword swinging down toward me. Right before I shut my eyes to await death, I saw a flash of movement out of the corner of my eye.

His screams of agony seemed to shake the room. In one swoop, Eoghanan fell to the ground in front of me. His body split open from temple to thigh. As he landed, a small glass bottle dropped from his hand and onto the floor, following the trail of his blood.

Chapter 44

In the instant Eoghanan hit the ground, I was given the time necessary to stand. I ran toward Niall, thrusting the sword into the center of his chest. The impact of the metal against his ribs reverberated all the way to my bones, and the pain of it forced me to release my grasp on its handle. The jab brought Niall to his knees as he stared down at his bleeding center.

"The vial! Somebody give it to Baodan now." I couldn't be certain, but unless Eoghanan still carried the poison he stole from Niall, the liquid could be the antidote he worked on.

Kenna jumped to grab the vial, and I turned my attention to Eoghanan who gasped uncomfortably as blood poured from half of him. Mary and Rhona rushed to get bandanges. I crouched next to him, gathering his uninjured hand into my own. "Oh my God. What did you do that for? It was so stupid. So very, very stupid." The words came between gasps. I could scarcely see him through my tears. He lived, but the life in his eyes dwindled as he continued to bleed.

His eyes focused dimly at my words, and he moved his hand from my grasp to touch my stomach. "I told ye I would do anything for either ye or Baodan."

Blood from his face dripped into his mouth, and he coughed as it prohibited his breathing. My hands trembled uncontrollably, but I reached up to clean his mouth, forcing myself to examine the extensiveness of his wounds for the first time.

Thankfully, his head wounds were not deep enough to cause damage. The gash that extended down the rest of his body worried me greatly. Although I was no doctor, I was fairly certain that the blade missed any vital organs. Still, I could see little hope of survival. His wounds could be closed, but infection would set in. In an area that large, it would kill him quickly. Eoghanan's eyes drifted closed as he lost consciousness and, for a brief moment, I tore my gaze away from him and looked up at the dying Niall.

Now collapsed onto his back, he choked on his own blood. My aim was poor enough so that his death was a slow one, and I was glad for it. He lay dying in a room full of people and not a one paid him any attention.

Mary stepped in front of my line of vision as she called to Eoin and Arran to help her lift Eoghanan.

"We will need to wrap the cloth around his whole body. No one will be able to close him until we have stopped the bleeding."

"Do you know what you're doing?" Not that it mattered, she was doing her best to help and that's all any of us could do.

"No, lass. No one here is a healer. I could be doing him more harm than good for all I know, but 'tis all I can think to do."

I nodded, standing from my crouched position next to him. "I know." I turned, unable to bear the thought of the lifeless Baodan who I knew lay behind me.

Instead, Baodan tried to sit up, extending his arm out to me as I ran to him.

"Oh God, it worked!" I grabbed either side of his face, smothering him in kisses until he reached his hand up to pull me away. "Slow down, lass, I am no leaving ye now. There will be time for that later. Did ye kill him?"

He no longer moved. As Bri nodded in answer to Baodan's question, I knew. "Yes."

"Good. That's me sweet, fiery lass."

The pain of moving roused Eoghanan into consciousness, and his moans caused Baodan to leap to his feet in alarm. "What happened to him?"

"After you fell, Niall ran toward me. Eoghanan jumped in front of him."

"He has saved us both, lass."

"I know." My voice broke again, and Baodan wrapped his arms around me.

"Will he live?" He directed his question to no one in particular and none knew the answer. I didn't see how he could, not with the extent of his injuries. We had nothing to provide protection against deadly infection.

Something hard thumped against my thigh. I glanced up at Baodan, thinking he wished to get my attention. "What was that?"

"What was what?"

"Did you touch me?" I reached down to the spot where I'd felt the touch and gasped at the object within my grasp.

"Are ye injured, lass?"

Wrapping my hand around the object, I pulled out the black stone and held it up for Baodan to see. "The rock. Get something for him to float on. We need to send him to Morna."

Chapter 45

"Hey. E-o. Can you open your eyes for me just a second? I know you want to sleep, but it's important that you look at me, okay?" My hand lay on his forehead, and I traced the top of his brow with my thumb. Slowly his eyelids flickered open.

"That is no me name, lass."

I smiled, my faith that he would be fine stronger than ever. Life remained in him, and Morna would heal him. "I know, but…"

He interrupted me before I could say more. "I know. I told ye I would teach ye how to say it when I needed a smile. I am verra much in need of a smile now."

He needed to be on his way, but I couldn't bring myself to deny him. I figured a lifted spirit would heal better than a sad one. "Okay. Teach me."

"Say 'yo,' then 'wun,' and 'en.'"

I tried to repeat him. I thought it sounded pretty good until the left side of his face pulled up into an amused smile. "I knew 'twould make me smile. Wretched job, lass."

"Yeah, well, I'll work on it while you're away."

He blinked his eye to symbolize a nod. "Aye, do. Just where is it that I am going?"

How could I explain to him when I knew how impossible it was to believe until you'd experienced it? "Do you trust me?"

"Aye. If Baodan does, so do I. I am proud to call ye sister."

"Good. I always wanted a little brother." I winked, he was

older than me. Centuries older. "I'm going to leave it to the person I'm sending you to to explain everything. Just know that you'll be taken care of, and you'll be better in no time."

"Then, let me be gone for I doona feel so well now."

"Ok." I bent and kissed him gently on the forehead. "But I think Baodan wants to say something to you first."

Baodan stepped in front of me, taking his brother by the hand. "Blood or no, ye are more a brother to me than Niall ever was. I'm sorry that I went so long with no treating ye as such. I hope that when ye return, things will be as they once were. Me love will be with ye every moment ye are away."

"And mine with ye."

We stepped away, and Eoin and Arran placed the makeshift raft atop the water, the stone placed on top of his stomach. He drifted gently into the center of the pond and vanished.

* * *

The sun rose as Baodan and I entered our bedchamber, but it did not stop us from crawling into bed. Despite the weariness of our bones and the heavy weight of our hearts, the feeling of clear relief spread throughout the castle. Tomorrow was sure to be a better day.

"Is yer neck badly hurt, lass?"

I felt nothing. Compared to Eoghanan's wounds, it was a scratch. "Not at all." I snuggled into the crook of my husband's arm, reaching for his hand as I smiled up at him. "I...I don't know if this is the right time, and I very well may be wrong but..."

"What is it, lass? I canna bear anything else bad."

"It's not bad." I pushed his fingers open and placed the

palm of his hand against my still-flat stomach and waited patiently for him to make the connection.

"No?"

I nodded, grinning at the smile that spread wide across his face. "I don't know and I won't for a few more weeks, but it's possible."

"A bairn? Mine?"

I smacked him lightly on the chest. "Is that a real question?"

He laughed, realizing the connotation of what he'd said. "Ach, no o'course it isna. 'Tis only I dinna think…"

He was cute when speechless. "It never crossed your mind? You know, that's what happens when you make whoopee."

"Ah, another one of yer strange words. Aye, I know what happens. 'Tis only I'm so happy I doona know what to say. Do ye think? Will it hurt the bairn if we make 'whoopee' again?"

I laughed at the ridiculousness of the word coming from his lips, reaching so that my lips could touch his. "No, the maybe-baby will be fine."

We found solace in each other's arms. As the sun beat down outside, we spent the next day wrapped in one another, our hearts brimming with the happiness that comes from safely holding the one you love most in all the world.

Epilogue

"A man left this for ye in the village."

The messenger extended a letter in my direction, bewilderment etched on his brow. The envelope was entirely modern. "Who left it?" Surely, Morna hadn't traveled back herself.

"I doona know. No one seemed to remember actually, but the man who gave it to me said that it must reach ye at once."

"I see. Thank you." My hands fidgeted on the envelope until the man retreated. I ripped it open once he was gone from sight.

I took in the words quickly, running to find Baodan to give him the long awaited news of his brother. I moved so quickly, I passed him in the grand entryway, only stopping at the sound of his voice.

"Mitsy, slow down before ye fall and break yer neck. Ye are no graceful enough to run in a dress. Doona dizzy the wee bairn, please."

We confirmed my suspicions about the pregnancy a few weeks after we sent E-o to Morna.

"Look! I told you E-o would be fine, although she says his scars will remain. In my book that's a small price to pay for his life. She hopes that he will be well enough to return home by the time the baby is born and…"

Baodan's eyes widened as he read the words I was about to tell him, "she doesn't seem to think he'll be returning home alone."

About the Author

Bethany Claire is the author of the Scottish, time-traveling romance novels *Morna's Legacy Series,* which includes her debut novel *Love Beyond Time, Love Beyond Reason,* a Christmas novella - *A Conall Christmas*, and her latest work, *Love Beyond Hope*. She lives in the Texas Panhandle.

Connect with me online:

http://www.bethanyclaire.com

http://twitter.com/BClaireAuthor

http://facebook.com/bethanyclaire

http://www.pinterest.com/bclaireauthor

If you enjoyed reading *Love Beyond Hope*, I would appreciate it if you would help others enjoy this book, too.

Recommend it. Help other readers find this book by recommending it to friends, readers' groups and discussion boards.

Review it. Please tell other readers why you like this book by reviewing it at Amazon or Goodreads. If you do write a review, please send me an email to bclaire@bethanyclaire.com so I can thank you with a personal email. Or visit me at http://www.bethanyclaire.com

JOIN THE BETHANY CLAIRE NEWSLETTER!

Sign up for my newsletter to receive up-to-date information of books, new releases, events, and promotions.

http://bethanyclaire.com/contact.php#mailing-list

Acknowledgments

As always, many thanks to my family. Your endless love and support mean the world to me.

To Dee, thank you for your wonderful suggestions and unwavering patience as I changed the send date over and over.

Mom, I have no words to express how grateful I am for you.

Thanks to my other team members: xuni.com, damonza.com, and Rik Hall formatting.

Books by Bethany Claire

Morna's Legacy Series

Love Beyond Time

Love Beyond Reason

Love Beyond Hope

A Conall Christmas – A Christmas Novella

Love Beyond Measure

(Available Summer 2014)

Re-discover the book that started it all....

Enjoy this sample of

Love Beyond Time (Book 1 of Morna's Legacy Series)

Chapter 1

Austin, TX

Present Day

Sun beamed against the windows as I walked down the line of tiny faces peering up at me. I knelt before each one, holding up a number between one and ten on my fingers, looking over each little body to ensure that laces were tied, backpacks on, and lunchboxes were in hand as I waited for their answer. As each called out the right number with a prideful smile, I gave them their daily sticker and moved on to the next student.

I could see Anthony three students down, pestering the unfortunate Harrison, who was standing in front of him and blowing in his ears every time he turned around to face the direction of the line. As Grace called out number seven and asked for help with her laces, I threw my most stern *cut it out* look in Anthony's direction. The ornery-but-exceedingly-bright child caught my meaning and returned the look with a sheepish grin as he stepped away from Harrison and stood still as a statue.

Two students later, I stood in front of Anthony. He rattled off the number nine that I was holding up in front of him before I even had a chance to look him over. Both laces were undone, and he had split his zipper so that only the middle of his jacket was actually closed.

"Good job Anthony! Here's your sticker. Still haven't mastered the old shoelaces yet, I see?"

"No, Ms. Mothgomfrey. I been working and working at it, but I just can't seem to get that rabbit to go around the hole."

I repressed an eye roll as I bent to tie his shoes. Anthony's speech was better than all of the other kindergarteners in his class, and I knew he could say my name, Ms. Montgomery, without problem, but he just lived for the giggles of all the other students every time he said my name that way.

"Well, those rabbits can be tricky that way, but you just keep working at it. You'll get it soon."

"I sure will! I promise! I sure am tired of watching you tie my shoes every day. Ya know, I'm five years old, it's humilly-aten."

"Well, Anthony. That's sure a big word. Where'd you hear that?"

"That's what my Mama said to Daddy the other day. She said it was humilly-aten to be married to a man that thought it was okay to watch television all day long on Sundays while she cleaned and cooked and did laundry and that he needed to get his fat, lazy a . . ."

The bell rang, interrupting his speech and saving the day as far as I was concerned. I should've seen that coming. I knew better than to ask Anthony an open-ended question.

I quickly checked the last few in line and went to the front of the classroom, motioning for the day's leader, Izzy, to hold open the door while everyone walked outside. Once everyone was out of the classroom and Izzy had returned to her place in the front of the line, I led them down the hallway, smiling at the sound of their tiny, squeaky shoes as they pitter-pattered single-file behind me.

* * *

Twenty minutes later, when the last child had been picked up, I shut the door to my classroom and plopped ungracefully down at my desk. I gently pressed my fingertips against my eyelids in an effort to push away the day's stress. It seemed to help a little, so I stood up, stretching mildly before I tucked my long, dark hair, which was now frizzing after being out in the wind, behind my ears.

I pushed my chair in and circled the room for a quick sweep before I headed home. I bent over every few feet to pick up the various crayons, chunks of Play-Doh, and construction paper scattered across the carpet. I knew the custodian would come along behind me shortly, but I just couldn't bear for her to see the classroom in this state of dishevelment. As I looked over the mess that scattered from one work center to another, I thought to myself, not for the first time today, how glad I was that I had decided against adding finger-painting to the day's lesson plans.

With my arms filled to capacity with various craft litter, I deposited the load into the trash can next to my desk. With a glance around the room, I decided I was satisfied enough to call it a day.

I stacked the handwriting exercises for the letter "G" on top of my desk to grade first thing Monday morning, and I was buttoning my jacket when my classroom aide Mitsy opened the door and stepped inside.

"Are you ready for your big date tonight? I talked to Brian and he said Daniel is super-excited!"

I spun quickly to face her, panic settling in my gut. "What? Oh, Mitsy, I totally forgot! Look. Maybe you could just call him and see if we could do it next Friday? You know, I'm really swamped right now. We'd both have more fun if we did it when I wasn't so distracted."

Mitsy placed her hands on both hips and narrowed her eyes as she spoke to me again, "I will do no such thing! And if you think you are going to get out of yet one more date, well, let me tell you, Miss I-have-no-problem-dying-alone, I am not going to let you weasel out of this one! He's a great guy, Bri. I haven't actually met him, but Brian's known him all of his life. His wife died two years ago, and he needs to get out of the house just about as badly as you need to. Just look at it as something that will benefit you both."

I turned away from her as I closed the coat closet and walked back over to my desk to grab my purse. "I'm not trying to weasel out of it. I just really need to work on lesson plans for next week, and I think I'm catching a cold."

Mitsy blocked the door to the classroom and grabbed my wrist as she dragged me back over to the filing cabinet beside my desk. I knew what she was about to grab before she opened the cabinet.

"You are not catching a cold, and don't you dare try to tell me that you have lesson plans to work on." I watched as she paused briefly to yank open the first drawer. "Let's see. What do we have here? All of Monday's lesson plans in this folder? Check. Tuesday? Check. Wednesday? Check. Do I really need to go on, Bri? You should just make it easier on yourself and tell me you're going, because you are either way. All there's left for you to decide is how soon you want me to get out of your hair." She smiled sweetly and placed my folders back into the cabinet, slamming the drawer shut with immense satisfaction.

Reluctantly I grinned and held my hands up in surrender. "Fine. Fine. I'll go. But you're going to let me pick out my own bridesmaid's dress for you and Brian's wedding, right?

Mitsy thrust her hand in my direction, "Deal."

* * *

I'd just zipped up the back of my dress when the doorbell rang at 7:30. *At least he's punctual,* I thought as I tried to put an earring on with one hand while attempting to slip myself into my heels with the other.

Taking a quick glance in the mirror, I slathered on some lip gloss, held my hand in front of my face to check my breath, and headed to answer the front door.

Daniel held a bouquet of flowers so that they covered his face, and as he slowly lowered them I had to swallow the audible gasp that crept up my throat. I was able to manage a polite, "Hello. Please come in," as my eyes combed over the thick, gray hair that covered his head.

As he made his way through the doorway I spotted a few

thick, wiry hairs sticking out from the opening in his ear, and the abnormally large nose that some men get when they age was evident from his profile.

He was handsome . . . for a man in his sixties. As I shut the front door, I found myself wishing I'd had that glass of wine I'd thought about when I got home from work.

Steeling myself, I turned to face him. "It's nice to meet you. The flowers are lovely. Thank you. Why don't I go put them in some water, and then we can leave?"

He extended them to me and as he grinned slightly, I could see that his eyes looked exceedingly kind. "I can tell I wasn't exactly what you were expecting. I guess Brian and Mitsy didn't tell you much."

I walked quickly into the kitchen, keeping my back to him so that he couldn't see my face as I spoke. "No, not too much. I know that you're a dentist and are related to Brian. I assumed you were a cousin."

The old man chuckled slightly, and his cheeks reddened as I walked back toward him. "My sons are his cousins. I'm his uncle."

"Oh." I stared down at my purse awkwardly, wishing I actually had something to look for inside it.

"Look. I don't want to make you uncomfortable, but we've both gotten all dressed up. Why don't we go ahead and go out to eat and visit with each other a little bit, then I'll bring you back here and we'll forget this whole thing ever happened. No harm, no foul. What do you say?"

He extended a hand in my direction, and sympathy washed through me as I reached to take it. He obviously had no more idea of what he was getting himself into than I did. "Good food, nice company. What could it hurt? Let's get out of here."

As he held the front door open, I walked straight into the person walking rather purposefully toward my front door.

"Mom?" I said.

* * *

I repeated myself for good measure as the uncomfortable feeling of shock ran down my spine for the second time. "Mom? What are you doing here? You're supposed to be in D.C., aren't you?"

She stepped back so that we could look at each other from a more appropriate distance, "Well, I'm happy to see you too, Bri. I'm glad I caught you before you left. I don't have a key to your new place. We need to talk right away. I have some very exciting news!"

I watched as she bounced up and down, the same thirteen-year-old trapped in a fifty-year-old's body that she'd always been. I knew the exact instant she spotted Daniel, still holding the door wide open, watching the spectacle.

As her eyes widened, she stopped bouncing, and immediately went into flirt mode; another one of my mother's classic qualities. "Well, hello sir. And who might you be?" She slowly stretched a hand in his direction.

"Name's Daniel. I was just leaving." He paused to pat me on the back and then walked through the door. "It was nice to meet you, Bri. I'll see you at the wedding."

I waved politely in his direction and ushered my mother inside, shutting the door behind me. She spun on me just as I'd latched the door.

"Who was that? Very handsome, but a little old for you, don't you think, dear?"

I leaned against the back of the door and exhaled loudly. "Very long story, Mom. But remind me that I need to have a conversation with Mitsy about what exactly it is that she thinks my standards are."

She laughed, obviously understanding the situation. "Well, seems like she understands my standards just fine. Do you have his phone number?"

I rolled my eyes and made my way into the living room. "No, Mom, I don't, but I'm sure Mitsy will give it to you if you want. Now, what's going on? Is everything okay?"

We sat down on the couch facing each other, and Mom excitedly reached for my hand as she told me her news.

"I got the grant!"

I couldn't help but smile at the excited expression on her face, "The grant to resume your work on Conall Castle? That's great, Mom!"

She squealed as she continued, "Yes, Bri, that grant. It's been nearly twenty years, but I'm finally going to get to go back and figure out what really happened."

My mother, Adelle Montgomery as most people knew her, was a world-renowned archaeologist. Her big break had come while working on an excavating project near the remains of Conall Castle in Scotland.

The tragedy of Conall Castle was one of the most well-known legends in Scottish history, and the mystery behind the destruction of the Conall clan had remained unsolvable for over four hundred years.

Within weeks of beginning her first lead dig at the ruins, Mom had discovered an underground library that, due to the strong stone base of the castle, had survived the infamous fire. It took weeks for Mom and her team to dig their way into the library, but once inside, they found countless archaeological treasures that had brought Adelle into the forefront of archaeology. Dozens of journals, hundreds of letters, and countless documents detailing family lineage with birth, death, and marriage certificates were all found within the library.

The find had propelled her career into overdrive. While the documents found in the basement shed a great light on the mysterious clan, none of the documents had solved the mystery of who had murdered the Conalls, afterwards burning the ancient castle to the ground.

After years of unsuccessfully solving the mystery, she moved on from her work on the Conall dig to other projects that sent her all over the world during the past twenty years; all the while she had been hoping for a reason to resume her work on Conall Castle.

"And I haven't told you the best part!" She squeezed my hand and bounced up and down like my kindergarteners before recess.

I sat quietly, waiting for her to tell me; knowing it would drive her crazy.

She stopped bouncing. "Aren't you going to say, 'what'?"

I laughed and indulged her. "What's the best part?"

"You're going to Scotland with me! I've already registered you as my assistant on the dig."

I jerked up off the couch, hitting the coffee table and sloshing water out of the cup that sat in front of me. "What? You know I can't. I have school. I teach kindergarteners. That's like asking a substitute to walk straight through the gates of Hell!"

"Oh, hush! You exaggerate. You haven't taken a personal day since you started teaching six years ago. I know you have a ton of days built up. Besides, we'll only be gone a couple of weeks. And you have Mitsy. Your students will be fine. You know you've always wanted to go to Scotland."

I reached up and squeezed the bridge of my nose with my fingers. Last minute travel plans did not appeal to me at all, but she was right about one thing. "I have always wanted to go to Scotland."

"Great! I'm going to go book our flights now. We leave Sunday."

Before I could put up a fight, she was on her way back to her car to grab her computer. Recognizing I'd been beaten, I walked back into the entryway and sank down beside the front door next to my school bag. Reaching inside, I grabbed my planner and tried to figure out what I was going to tell my principal.

Chapter 2

Scotland

1645

The eldest Conall brother paced back and forth outside his father's chambers, reluctant to leave his father's side but understanding the laird's desire to speak to his youngest son alone. After what seemed like hours Eoin heard the door begin to creak, and Arran Conall emerged from their father's room.

Standing at over six foot four, Arran was still at least two inches shorter than Eoin. With blond hair that fell to his shoulders and vibrant blue eyes, Arran was very popular with the lasses of Conall Keep.

Although Eoin knew his own good looks were a fair rival to his brother's, he was careful not to earn such a reputation for frivolous lovemaking. His younger brother, however, embraced his reputation; it was a rare night that his bed was empty, and even rarer that the same woman was found there twice.

Arran's carefree nature and love of life were contagious, and there were few times when Eoin had seen his brother without a smile. But this time, when he exited their father's room, Arran's smile was gone. The red tip of his nose and the strain in his eyes revealed that Arran was too proud to let the flood of tears flow.

Knowing any attempt to comfort would only embarrass him further, Eoin looked at the ground as he entered their father's chamber. Eoin had been only five when his mother passed away while giving birth to Arran, and all Eoin remembered about her was spending afternoons in her beloved garden, watching her tend the plants with exquisite care.

His father, on the other hand, had been his constant companion. Eoin was the spitting image of his father: same long, dark hair and ebony eyes; same quiet-yet-confident demeanor, so different from his brother's loud and boisterous way of life. As children, Eoin and Arran depended on their father for everything, and although his father had spent the past thirty years preparing him, Eoin had never expected to be laird of Conall Castle so soon.

He would have done anything to prevent his father's fate, but as his gaze fell upon the laird, Eoin knew there was nothing to be done. While he had been thrown from horses many times in his life, the fall his father had taken that morning tossed his aging body onto a rocky hillside. The damage inflicted was too much for his body to heal. His father was dying, and all Eoin could do now was sit at his bedside and comfort him during his last minutes.

* * *

Alasdair prepared to impart his final wish upon his eldest son as he watched him enter the room. He tried to sit up as Eoin approached his bedside. The thought of his heir seeing him in such a weakened state pained him almost as much as the crushed ribs and deflated lung that forced his breath to come in short rasps. He was a warrior, built strong like both his sons. He found it difficult to believe that it would be a creature as gentle as a horse that would send him to his deathbed, but he supposed that was just another sign that while the body and mind age, the soul often remains oblivious to fragile bones, creaking joints, and moments of forgetfulness.

Despite grayed hair and failing body, Alasdair knew in his heart he was still the youthful, handsome lad who wanted nothing more than to steal another kiss from his beloved wife. It had been twenty-five years since Elspeth passed away, and he still couldn't think of her without tears springing up in his dark eyes.

He pushed thoughts of her away, for he knew he would see his beloved soon enough. As his son sat down beside him, Alasdair allowed his thoughts to drift to the burden he knew he must place upon Eoin's shoulders.

Alasdair would not tell his son the true reason for his insistence upon a marriage between Eoin and Blaire MacChristy. For while he knew the true nature of Morna's predictions, Eoin had never known the witch. Alasdair knew if his dying wish for his son was based on some crazed long-dead aunt's predictions, it would only make Eoin even more resistant to the marriage.

It had long been believed that his son's betrothal to Blaire was to ensure the protection of the MacChristy territory. Donal MacChristy was laird over the smallest castle and territory in Scotland. With poor people and few provisions for safety, the MacChristy clan was ever in need of help from neighboring allies. It had been great fortune that Alasdair had always been good friends with Donal as it had made arranging the betrothal that much easier and more believable.

Alasdair knew that if Morna's predictions and spell came true, Blaire MacChristy would soon be replaced with a lass from the twenty-first century, and he was certain Eoin would not remain oblivious to the strange happenings. To help ease his son's shock, Alasdair had ensured that all of Morna's journals detailing her prediction, spell, and wish could be found in the witch's beloved secret room in the castle's basement, along with the spelled plaque showing Blaire's picture. He had also told the prediction and story to his beloved housemaid, Mary, but he wasn't sure if she'd believed his outrageous tale.

After Morna's death, Alasdair had discovered her journals detailing the enchanted plaque and how she planned for the swap to take place. The identity spell had already been set before Morna passed. Regardless of what happened, there would be a girl born many years from now, identical in appearance to Blaire MacChristy. The exchange of the two girls hinged upon the plaque Morna placed in the center of her sanctuary. If both Blaire and the identical girl were to see and read the words on the plaque out loud during some point in their lives, their paths would combine, and they would switch places in time. This part of Morna's plan was entirely dependent upon fate, and Alasdair strongly doubted if any such fantastic occurrence would ever take place. Regardless of his misgivings, he refused to betray his sister's memory.

"Son," Alasdair's chest began to weigh down on itself, begging him not to say anymore, but he refused to let his body fail before he said his peace, "I doona want ye and Arran to mourn me for long. I have had a full life. Everything I ever wanted, I have possessed."

"I don't want to hear ye say another word about that, Father. Just get some rest, and ye will feel much better come morning."

"Ye can hold your lies, son. My body may be weak, but my mind is sharp. Ye know as well as I do that I am dying. I need ye to make peace with that as well. For I expect ye to continue with the wedding plans as if nothing has happened. Ye will be laird of Conall Castle within the hour. It falls to ye to watch over not only our territory but the MacChristy's as well, by marrying Blaire."

* * *

Dread crept up Eoin's spine at the thought of going through with his marriage to Blaire, but he refused to dwell on such things right now. He had never argued or denied his father anything, and he certainly wasn't going to start tonight.

"I want ye to send word to Laird MacChristy come sun up. Suggest that Blaire come to reside here at once, so that ye can make yer preparations together. I believe the wedding should be set for three weeks' time. I know she tries yer patience, but I expect ye to treat and cherish her as I did yer mother."

Eoin didn't believe himself capable of showing anyone the kind of adoration that his father had shown his mother. He didn't really think anyone other than his father was capable of loving that deeply, especially not himself. Despite having had significantly fewer partners than Arran, he was no less talented at lovemaking. But he had never met a lass who made him, even for a moment, dread spending the rest of his life without her.

He would not tell his father that, so instead, just as Alasdair Conall took his last breath and left this world to meet his beloved Elspeth once more, Eoin vowed, "I promise Father. I promise to marry her, and I promise to try."

Made in the USA
San Bernardino, CA
21 March 2016